The Bishops' Struggle

Book One
The Bishops' Resolve Series

Timothy Patrick Means

Mad Dog Publications

The Bishops' Struggle
Book One of The Bishops' Resolve Series
Copyright 2023 by Timothy Patrick Means

ISBN 978-1-7376017-6-0
All rights reserved
Printed in the United States of America

This book is a work of fiction. Names, characters, places, and incidents are either a product of the author's imagination or are used fictitiously. Any resemblance to actual events, persons, or locales, living or dead, is purely coincidental.

Published by
Mad Dog Publications
Boise, Idaho

www.timothypatrickmeans.com

Cover by M.Y. Cover Design

To the new discoverer of my writings, to the brave ones who purchased these written pages and look inside, and to the pioneer seeking more adventurers: Climb on board and take this journey together.

Thank you.

A Note from the Author

The Bishops' Struggle is the first in a series of three books in The Bishops' Resolve Series. It is the next evolution in the story told in The Bishops' Sacrifice Series.

While each book is a stand-alone story, various characters, along with their back story, mentioned in each may make it more fun to read them all in order, along with The Sterling Chronicles, *a book of short stories about psychic detective Sterling.*

The Bishops' Sacrifice Series

Book 1: The Demon Shadow
Book 2: The Family Curse
Book 3: The Guardian Alliance

The Sterling Chronicles

Chapter 1

A LINE OF CARS SLOWLY moved past the cemetery gates, stopping along the curb near a lonely gravesite. Car doors opened, and the numerous mourners, dressed in black, unfurled their umbrellas as the spring rain steadily descended. Melissa's face was wet from tears even before she stepped into the shower as she wept for her mother. This day marked the final entry on the life of Barbara Bishop Harding. Ovarian cancer hadn't been discovered until it was too late. At stage four malignancy, nothing could be done to stop the advancing killer that took this mother's life.

Melissa's twin sons, Mark and David, stared out the rain-washed windows, observing crowds gathering at the gravesite. The attendants from the funeral home set the single casket above the dark hole that would be the final resting place for their grandmother. A large canvas tarp covered the coffin. A small podium with a series of folding chairs was lined up in two rows and housed under a tent just large enough to keep the worst of the rain off a dozen mourners.

Just then, Rachel's familiar Cadillac pulled past the gate. Seeing that her younger sister had arrived, Melissa thought it was time that she and her husband, Dan Carpenter, join the rest of the family. Popping open their umbrellas, she herded her family out of their minivan.

Once outside, they stood briefly, solemnly waiting until Rachel, her husband, Eric Cooper, and their two daughters, six-year-old Sara and eight-year-old Kathy, joined them.

Melissa hugged her sister lovingly. "I regret this day!"

"So do I, sis, but we both knew it would come."

"Yes, I suppose."

"Have you seen Dad yet?" Rachel asked, fighting back the tears.

"He called me to say he was running late."

Seeing the crowds gathering around the gravesite, Dan announced, "Perhaps we all should get to our seats before the service begins."

Receiving silent nods from everyone, Melissa quickly took hold of her sister's arm for support. Walking together to the gravesite, they sat on the plastic chairs.

Seated across the casket decorated with beautiful roses, their mother's favorite, Melissa began to cry again. She already missed her mother badly. She and Rachel cried together as they held hands, sharing in the sense of loss.

Melissa's twin sons stared silently at the ground with nothing to say. At the age of thirteen, they witnessed the complete breakdown of their mother after the news of their grandmother's cancer. They wanted to help. They loved their mother. But what could thirteen-year-old boys understand of the pain and loss their mother felt?

They tried to be quiet, help around the house, and get their homework done without bothering their mother while she spent countless hours at the hospital with their grandmother. Those endless, tedious hours of sitting in a hospital waiting room, sometimes tasked with keeping their younger cousins Sarah and Kathy out of mischief, had been about as boring as two active thirteen-year-olds could stand.

It was over now. Their dad had promised things would return to normal after the funeral. They had loved their grandmother. They didn't want to see her suffer. They didn't want to watch their mom grieve but anxiously hoped for the "good old days" to return.

The boys, drilled in polite behavior, stood to their feet to allow the adults to pass. A familiar voice spoke behind them, and the twins turned to see their grandfather, Mark, appear. Another man, one they had never seen before, walked with him.

Melissa and Rachel stood and tenderly embraced Mark. Eyeing her father through swollen red eyes, Melissa asked, "Dad, how are you holding up?"

"Oh, I don't know. As good as can be expected."

"We both know this is hard for you, but you must realize that Mom is no longer in pain. She is in a much better place."

"No, you're right, but it's just so hard. I miss your mom terribly."

"We all do; this is hard for all of us," Rachel said.

"Sterling, Oh, I'm so glad you came," Melissa cried out as she noticed the man beside her dad.

"You don't think I would have missed saying goodbye to your mother, do you?" He answered with the sound of sadness in his voice.

"It looks like the service is about to begin so we should take our seats," Mark said.

"Father, why not sit here between Rachel and me?"

"What about Sterling?" Mark asked.

"We'll make room," Dan said, directing his sons to

move down a few seats.

The family settled, and the service began.

Mark, seated between his two daughters, reached over to grab both their hands. He glanced at his wife's casket. The thought of not seeing her ever again hit suddenly. A feeling of loss overwhelmed him; he was lonelier than he had ever imagined. Tears flowed down his cheeks as his daughters wrapped their arms around him.

Rachel reached into her purse to get a tissue and handed it to her father. He thanked her as he slowly wiped away his tears.

Staring at the white casket that held his wife's remains, Mark asked himself, *How did it come to this? She was much too young to die!*

The priest appeared carrying his Bible, stood before the casket, and announced, "Would everyone please have a seat? The service is about to begin."

After several minutes, the crowd became silent, and a hush fell over them.

The priest said, "We are gathered here today to say our final farewells to a loving woman named Barbara Bishop Harding."

Those words were the only thing that Melissa remembered hearing that day. Everything else was a complete blur, soon to be forgotten. What remained was how their mother's determination to stay alive seemed interminable. Melissa could only hope to be so brave when facing adversity, but she wasn't like her mother; no, when difficulties became too much for her to handle, she sought other forms of dealing with her problems. But all that was in the past. She wouldn't turn to drugs or alcohol again.

After the funeral service, the wake was held at

Rachel's house. A large gathering of family and friends arrived to remember their mother. Her Uncle Butch was recently released from prison. He gave a long speech, telling many stories about his sister when they were younger, then eventually broke down and cried, admitting to everyone that he was sorry for not being there when Barbara needed him most. *Did the alcohol he consumed make his regret that much more meaningful?* Melissa wondered. *Or less?*

People continued arriving, including a blonde woman no one had seen before. It wasn't until she walked up to Rachel to introduce herself that her identity was discovered.

"My name is Marsha Marks. We have never met before, but I'm Jacob's wife. I'm sorry he isn't here to give his condolences. He wanted to come but couldn't because he's working on an important case. Jacob often spoke of your mother as one of the most courageous women he ever met."

Rachel's response was warm and thoughtful. "Thank you for coming. We're sorry Jacob couldn't make it."

Although they hadn't seen Jacob in years, Rachel and Melissa were grateful to him for helping to free them from the hands of a kidnapper.

"I had heard he had become a policeman," Rachel said.

"Yes, he always says that helping to free you from Tommy Taylor was one of the things that smade him want to join the police force. He says that experience turned his life around," the woman replied.

"Well, I guess something good came of it then," Rachel said.

She was glad when another visitor arrived, and she

could end the uncomfortable conversation. Reliving those awful days when first Melissa, then she, had been held captive by Tom Taylor and his family was just too much to ask for today.

The new arrival was an old friend, one both Melissa and Rachel were pleased to see, someone who had been a pillar of strength to them over the years, notably while their mother's health declined. Now in her eighties, Susan Bernstein seemed determined that age wouldn't slow her down. She embraced both sisters and fought the tears masked behind her warm smile.

Heather Janson also came over to talk with Susan. Heather was Tom Taylor's sister, and people who knew only part of the kidnapping story stared surprised to see her at the funeral.

But Rachel, Melissa, and their father were glad she was there. When her father, stepmother, and brother Tom had been ensorcelled by the dark wizard Tobias into kidnapping Melissa and Rachel, Heather defied her family and helped save the girls.

Rachel shook her head as she noticed how some people turned their backs on Heather. *If they only knew the real story*, she thought, then snorted softly to herself. Most people who heard the real story wanted to lock up Melissa and Rachel. That had been part of the reason Melissa had turned to drugs in her early twenties. It was hard to recover from trauma when no one understood what had happened.

Tobias, an evil sorcerer many hundreds of years old, had found a way to escape death. But while his consciousness remained active, he had no body—something he dearly wanted.

Finally, he found the means to resurrect himself by possessing the consciousness of one of his descendants,

Martin Taylor—Heather and Tommy's father. When Heather realized what was happening, she took a family heirloom, a valuable manuscript that described the curse that joined the Taylor and Bishop families, and showed it to Barbara.

With Heather's help, as well as Sterling's and several of his friends who were versed in magic and sorcery, Barbara could free her daughters. But before the sorcerer Tobias was defeated, he indoctrinated Tommy and made him his apprentice in magic. Martin and their stepmother, Elaine, had died at the hands of Tobias when they did not please him. And Tommy had killed all their sisters and brothers in a magical fire that destroyed their family.

Barbara had acted as a mother figure to Heather after the loss of her entire family. She came to live with them since she had nowhere else to go after everything was over. Both sisters had accepted her as family. They stayed close throughout the years and often spent the holidays together. When Barbara was ill, Heather often took her to her medical appointments when everyone was busy. Heather had been a devoted friend to Barbara, Rachel, and Melissa.

AFTER SOME TIME THE crowd began to thin as most people left for home. Only a few remained behind, including Heather, Sterling, and Susan. They comforted Mark and talked about how Barbara would be missed.

The doorbell rang. As Rachel watched, she saw her husband answer the door. A delivery driver handed him an enormous bouquet of black roses with a large black bow. He looked at his wife, unsure of what to do with them. Rachel quickly excused herself from speaking with her uncle, who still sat in a corner nursing a whiskey. She swiftly took the bouquet from Eric and disappeared into the kitchen.

"Who sent those ugly roses?" Melissa asked, appearing next to her side.

"I'm not sure, but I have a good guess."

Melissa saw a card was attached. "Let's find out, shall we?" Removing the card from the box, she quickly tore open the small envelope. Reading the sympathy card to herself, she crumpled it up a moment later and threw it in the trash can.

When Rachel saw her response, she put out her hand to stop her sister. "Wait, let me see it. I want to know what was written on the card that upset you."

"Sure, if you want. But let me warn you, you won't like it."

Taking the card in her hand, Rachel smoothed it out and read it aloud. "At last the bitch is gone. Now is the time for a joyful song. Shouting a curse over her grave, soon her spirit will be my slave."

"What a load of crap," Melissa said in disgust.

Rachel, without hesitation, turned on the gas flames of the stove and lit the card ablaze. As it burned it gave off a colorful display as the ink changed from a dark blue to orange and eventually to black ash. Taking the smoking remains over to the sink, Rachel turned on the faucet and drenched it before it burned her fingers. Afterward she pushed it down the garbage disposal.

Hearing the commotion in the kitchen, Susan Bernstein appeared. They explained what the card had said.

"The work of a sick-minded puke. Who on earth would be so callous as to send black roses at a time like this?"

Heather appeared in the doorway. "It's from Tom,

my brother; I'm sure of it. He has never forgiven your family for testifying at his hearing. But honestly, I never expected him to do something like this; it's too cruel. I keep hoping he will change."

Turning to Melissa and Rachel, she added, "You must believe me. I never imagined Tom would go this far. I stopped visiting him in prison five years ago when I saw the darkness growing inside him; I thought it best to avoid further contact."

"We don't blame you, Heather. It's not your fault Tom Taylor is your brother," Melissa said.

Melissa called her husband, Dan, who was talking with Sterling in the living room and asked if he had a moment. Dan quickly excused himself.

As he entered the kitchen, he asked, "So who sent the ugly roses?"

"We're not sure, but someone out there seems to have a morbid sense of humor. Who knows, and who cares?" Melissa said, not wanting to upset her husband.

He knew the whole story of her family and Tom Taylor—everyone in town seemed to know it or thought they did.

"Listen," said Melissa, "could you please be a dear and take these horrible-looking flowers outside and dump them in the trash?"

"Sure thing," he responded. Grabbing the arrangement of flowers, he carried them away.

Sterling, who had followed Dan into the kitchen, asked Melissa, "So do you know who sent them?"

Rachel quickly answered. "Yes, there was a card, if you want to call it that. But after I read it, I burned the damn thing and threw it down the garbage disposal."

"If you don't mind me asking, what did it say exactly?"

"Oh, some crap about singing a song now that my mother was gone, shouting a curse over her grave, soon her spirit is a slave," Melissa explained.

Sterling's expression grew concerned. "I don't like the sound of that."

"Come on, Sterling, how is it possible that anyone could hurt my mother now? She has passed away; she's now at peace," Rachel announced.

"Yes, you're right; Barbara is in a safe place, away from all the magical witchcraft. However, you can't help but think that someone seems to think they're powerful—especially believing they can enslave a person's soul. Personally, I can only think of one individual. Besides, I suddenly feel uneasy, as if a dark spirit is lurking about." Sterling said.

"We already know that Tom Taylor is a free man. I'll never understand how the parole board could let him go. But you never hear about him anymore in any of the newspapers. It's as though he fell off the planet. I think he has started a new life elsewhere, or at least that's what I would have done if I had been in prison all those years," Rachel said.

"Listen, I don't want Dad to hear about this, okay?" Melissa put in.

"Speaking of your father, where is he? I haven't seen him for several hours," Sterling announced.

"He told me he had to go home for something. He said he'd be back in a few minutes, but that was hours ago," Melissa explained.

Rachel suddenly looked concerned and suggested that Melissa call her father to see if he was all right.

"Sure. Hopefully, he didn't fall or break his hip." Reaching inside her purse, Melissa quickly dialed his number. After getting no response, she said, "He's not answering. I'm going to his house to see if he's okay."

"Let me come with you," Rachel suggested.

"If you don't mind, I'd like to go with you both," said Sterling.

"Perhaps that's a good idea. After all, if Dad did fall, we'll need your help getting him into the car," Rachel answered.

Having to get up early the following day, Dan gathered his sons and left for home.

The sisters waited outside and agreed to let Sterling drive them. Getting inside the BMW, they hurried away. A short time later they arrived at their father's house. They noticed his truck parked in the driveway. The place looked dark inside, as if no one was home. Parking the car directly behind Mark's truck, Sterling exited his vehicle. Walking back, he opened the trunk to remove a large flashlight. Turning on the light, they slowly approached the front door.

Now, even more concerned, Rachel and Melissa followed Sterling. Melissa yelled out for her father but got no response. When she tried to open the front door, she found it unlocked. Walking inside, she again called out to her father but heard nothing.

Inside nothing looked out of place. Melissa turned around and said, "This isn't good. Where's our father?"

Directing his light into the darkness, Sterling discovered the light switch and flipped it on. In the living room nothing seemed out of place. Stepping back toward the kitchen, he turned on the light.

"Oh my god, what happened to Dad?" Rachel screamed out after seeing the blood.

Chapter 2

In the kitchen they saw several chairs tipped over; the kitchen table had been knocked on its side, and the back door was pried open, barely hanging from one hinge. They saw blood droplets on the floor running back toward the back door.

"It looks like there was a struggle of some type. Notice the black scuff marks on the floor?" Sterling said. "And the blood droplets looked smeared. If the blood belongs to your father, then he didn't go without a fight. I can tell you that much."

"Why my father? He has never even hurt a fly. Why him?" Melissa cried, distraught. This disappearance was too much. First, her mom's death, the funeral. Now, her dad had been assaulted and maybe was missing.

"Yes, why?" Rachel cried, turning to Sterling for answers.

"Honestly, I haven't got a clue. Now listen to me, both of you. This is obviously foul play; we must call the police to report this at once." Sterling quickly dialed 911.

Within minutes two uniformed officers arrived at the house and took down all the pertinent information about what Mark was wearing, along with his age and a recent photo. Truthfully, nothing else was known except that Mark Harding had fought his attackers, possibly paying the price for his refusal to join them. Mark had type 1 diabetes so it was essential to maintain his sugar levels by taking his insulin regularly. This made the fact that he was missing even more concerning. How long did he have before he could fall into a coma?

As lab technicians arrived to go over the crime scene, the small kitchen became crowded. Sterling suggested that the two sisters follow him into the living room to have a seat until the police were ready to talk to them again.

"I should have seen this coming," Sterling said, not bothering to take a seat as he had suggested to the girls; instead, he paced in front of them. "I wasn't sure whether what I've been feeling was reality or not. A few days ago I suddenly felt a restlessness within my soul, like an evil intruder had invaded my inner sanctum."

"What do you mean an evil intruder?" Melissa asked. A chill ran down her spine. She remembered everything that had happened when she was kidnapped at age fifteen. She had seen and learned far more about the evils of this world and the supernatural world. It still haunted her nightmares.

"About a week ago I was alone in my apartment, determined to search out Stannis. I haven't heard from him in a while, and I've been worried," Sterling explained.

Stannis was a sorcerer skilled in white magic. He had been instrumental in helping Sterling and Barbara to save the girls when they had been kidnapped.

"It was getting late, well past midnight. The room suddenly became frigid, and a dark shadow appeared above me. My attempts were hampered as I tried to clear my mind to focus on the strange presence. What was in my room seemed content to play with me, as though it enjoyed seeing my inability and not comprehending its origin. I can tell you it was evil."

"In what way?" asked Rachel.

"It can be hard to explain, but yes, evil is what it felt like to me. Even as I focused on its purpose for entering my home, I occasionally saw a dark shadow sprint across the room, unhindered by physical restraints such as space or time. This thing would rise from the floor and then enter the ceiling above me, suddenly reappearing through the walls. The whole time it was just a blurry, dark shadow. After several minutes it disappeared entirely."

"What does this have to do with our father?" Rachel asked.

Sterling looked back toward the kitchen, reexamining the floor with the spilled blood droplets, and said, "Perhaps this is more than a simple break-in. I believe evil is involved in Mark's disappearance."

Sterling began to pace again. "I don't know why this is happening, damn it! I thought that once that Tobias creature was dead, all your lives would be free from this type of evil. Apparently, I was wrong; I fear some of the same forces are at work again, and we may need to overcome this same evil again."

"Tommy Taylor, that son of a bitch, is behind this. I just know it," Rachel said bitterly.

"Yes, I wouldn't be surprised if he was. After all, he hated every one of you. If you remember, at his trial the man promised to take revenge on the 'Bishop Bitches,' as he called you girls and your mother."

"Alright, Sterling, what now? How do we find Tommy Taylor? He disappeared after he got out of prison. Heather hasn't heard from him in years."

"First of all, Melissa, you must remember he is no

longer little Tommy Taylor, the teenager. Tom has carried with him years of loathing for your family. Instead, you'll find a man filled with vile hate. After almost twenty years behind steel bars, this man is an animal that had been kept in a cage. Now set free, who knows where he will strike next?"

"Fine, Tom then, if you prefer to call him that. Either way, I want him to be gone, far away, where he can no longer hurt my family; I have my twins and Rachel's girls to consider. Are they in even more danger than the twins? He always had a grudge against the women of the family."

"I don't think this new predicament we find ourselves in involves a need for sacrifice, as when you both were taken. No, not this time! I believe, instead, it's simply a need for revenge for how Tom's life ended," Sterling explained.

"I'm not surprised. Truthfully, I have dreaded this day, should it appear. Yes, this man hates us and wants us all dead, including you, Sterling! If I recall, you had a hand in defeating his master, Tobias," Melissa announced.

"I just wish I could wrap my hands around that guy's throat," said Rachel.

Melissa stared back into the kitchen where her father's blood was still sprinkled on the floor. "I can't believe he took our father."

"I can't either," Rachel agreed.

Joining her sister on the couch, they broke down, realizing the possibility that they might never see their father again.

Just then Melissa's cell phone rang. Reaching into her purse, she saw that it was her husband calling.

"Hello, honey," she answered quickly.

"Melissa, where are you? I'm worried and sick; you've been gone for several hours. What's wrong?"

"Dan, I can`t believe this is happening again." She paused, searching for the right words. She returned to the phone and cried, "Someone has kidnapped my father."

"What! Who would do such a thing?"

"We're not sure. Listen to me, darling, the police are here, along with the crime lab. We'll be home soon, Dan, I promise!"

"Alright, if you need me, I'll be there."

"Yes, of course, don't worry. I'll have Sterling drive us back home when we're finished here; I love you."

"I love you, too. Please be safe. I'll talk to you soon."

Just then a young detective walked into the house wearing a dark suit. His gold badge was on his belt. "I'm so sorry to hear the news about your father."

"Jacob Marks, oh thank heavens," Melissa cried, wiping away the tears on seeing the old friend, who had helped to free them when they were kidnapped years before.

"How are you two handling this? And on top of your mom's funeral. I'm sorry I couldn't make it, but I was on duty," Jacob said.

With irony, Rachel looked at him and said, "Well, after burying our mother and losing our father in one day, I suppose you could say we've been better."

"Jacob, it's good to see you." Sterling stepped up and shook the man's hand.

"Listen, I want all of you to know we're doing everything possible to find your father."

"We know you are," said Melissa. "I'm glad you're

here instead of someone we've never met—someone who knows us and about what happened before. It's nice having a person we know on the other side of the police work—someone we can trust. Please tell us what you've seen thus far. Can you tell us if our father is still alive?"

"So far we can only ascertain that there was quite a scuffle. Your father put up a good defense. To me, it looks like he was surprised by his attackers, who burst into the house through the back door," Jacob explained. "But I have work to do; let me get to it. I still have to talk with the crime lab investigators," Jacob responded. A moment later he disappeared back into the kitchen.

Another hour passed, and the crime lab had just finished examining blood splatters, looking for the subtlest of clues. Pictures of the broken back door were taken, along with it being dusted for fingerprints. Finally, Jacob returned to the living room as everyone stood to their feet, awaiting the bad news they knew was coming. A look of despair was written on each of their faces.

"Well, we can tell you that it looks like the home invaders gained access through the back door. We found marks on the door jamb made with some large, heavy object, no doubt a pry bar of some type."

"What about the blood splatters?" Sterling inquired.

"We'll have to leave that for the crime lab investigators. Melissa, we need some samples from the bathroom for DNA. Maybe your dad's comb or toothbrush?"

"Yes, certainly," she responded.

"There is something else. We found three distinctly different shoe marks on the floor, one large and two smaller prints. According to the smear marks on the floor, there was more than one attacker. We believe a man and two women executed the crime by the size of the shoe impressions."

"So what you're saying is that Tom Taylor has hired some thug and two women to act as co-conspirators?" Sterling replied.

"We don't know for sure it was Taylor," Jacob cautioned. "Although please believe me when I tell you he is the most reasonable suspect in this case at this very moment. In fact, I'm on my way to have a little chat with Taylor."

"You think you can find him? If you do, I hope you fry that bastard this time," said Rachel spitefully.

"Well, perhaps he will fry if found guilty, but for now he is just a suspect," Jacob continued. "Something else: Neighbors saw a dark-colored van with a plumber's logo on the door. They thought your father was having problems with his plumbing, the reason for the crashing noises."

"Yes, isn't that always the case? People nowadays still accept the obvious as the cause of disturbances and never think beyond what is visible. In this case, it would have been better for Mark if someone had investigated the noises they heard," Sterling announced.

"Listen, we're all done here. Why don't you ladies return home? I will call you if there is any break in the case," Jacob suggested.

"Jacob, I can't leave. Dad's house is open. What if some robber shows up to take everything that he owns?" Melissa responded.

"I'll make sure the house is locked tight; I promise you that." Reaching within his coat pocket, he withdrew his wallet. Removing a small business card, he handed it to Melissa, promising to contact her if he got a break in the case.

"Listen, why don't you two meet me at my car? I'll join you in a minute. I want to ask Jacob something." Sterling suggested.

"Sure, why not? We can't do anything else but wait," Rachel responded, leaving the house with her sister in tow.

Sterling turned to Jacob and said, "I see that you found something under the kitchen table. What was it, if you don't mind me asking?"

"Well, I didn't want to show it to the girls, you understand," Jacob remarked.

"Yes, of course."

Jacob removed something from his pants pocket and displayed a plastic bag with a red sticker marked "Evidence." Inside the bag was a human tooth. Looking up at Sterling, he said, "I believe it came from one of the attackers. It's a front tooth covered in a gold filling. Nowadays such a display of wealth is done by gang members or young guys trying to look cool, not men of Mark's age."

"You're probably right. If I were to guess, I would say that Mark Harding fought his attackers with all he had to give until he was overcome. All right, for now, I won't say anything about the tooth. But I believe you owe it to the girls to keep them informed of any news about their father," Sterling responded.

"I know. I will call them if I hear anything conclusive," Jacob said.

"Thanks, Jacob, I must run. We'll talk later."

Jacob stopped outside to smoke and watched Sterling hurry to his car and drive away. Inhaling smoke into his lungs, he took a few minutes to reminisce.

It seemed like a lifetime ago when the story broke

about Melissa's kidnapper, Tom Taylor. Although no one would believe this young kid could have been responsible for the kidnapping of the Harding girls and the murders of all his siblings except Heather, his father, and stepmother. Still, it was plastered in the local newspaper headlines that he was the one who killed them all. What was known was bad enough; if people had understood the full extent of the story, Tom would have been in a hole under the prison, not just locked up in it.

But once he did go to prison, society breathed a sigh of relief. And then he was set free. Considering the nature of his crimes, it was amazing that he had been paroled. The reason printed in the newspapers was that his young age at the time demanded he be given leniency. But Jacob had wondered when he heard the news. Had there been some other force at work to get Tom out of prison? And how many more murders would now be laid at Tom Taylor's feet until he was captured again?

The girls had told the officer who interviewed them about the black roses sent to Rachel's house this morning. It was obvious to Jacob that the roses and Mark's kidnapping were connected. It was also apparent that Tom was involved. It was up to Jacob to prove it.

Flicking his used cigarette butt on the front lawn, he returned to the dreadful scene of another Harding kidnapping—this time the father.

As STERLING DROVE BACK to Melissa's house, the women tried to mask their worry by talking of happier times. Melissa remembered when she and Rachel traveled to Europe for a vacation after the abduction. It was a marvelous time. But when they returned home, newspaper reporters hounded the family to the point of parking on their front lawn, searching for a story that would bring them fame. It took a long time until everything returned to normal.

When they returned to Melissa's home, all the lights were on. Sterling could see her husband, Dan, in the living room watching television inside the house. When they entered the front door, he stood and asked, "What did the police say happened to Mark? Do they know who took him?"

"No, I'm afraid not. We all know whoever took Dad burst through his back door. Supposedly, they were driving a plumbing van. The neighbors heard crashing noises but assumed the plumber was making all the racket," Melissa explained.

Turning to Sterling, Rachel asked, "Would you mind taking me home, please?"

"I can drive you; it won't be a bother, sis!" Melissa responded.

"No, I have to go that way so it won't be a problem," Sterling put in.

"Are you sure? I can have Melissa drive me."

"Listen, it's late; you and your sister have had a very trying day. You relax, and I'll take her home."

"Sure."

Walking over to hug her sister goodbye, Rachel turned to Sterling and said, "I'm ready; let's be off."

"I'll call you tomorrow to see if Jacob has discovered anything new."

Arriving at the car, they again extended their heartfelt gratitude to Sterling for all his help, and he and Rachel drove away. The words between them were few; Rachel seemed content to stare out the car window, remembering her father, rather than catching up on old times with the psychic who had been her mother's friend, not hers.

It was not to be unexpected. After all, over the years little in the way of communication was ever shared between them. It wasn't as though he was ever invited to come to dinner during the holidays or perhaps a Christmas card. His life was hectic, with new criminal cases piling in every week. It didn't allow him free time to indulge in such things, but he never forgot about the family he helped bring back together.

With directions to Rachel's house uttered every so often, they soon arrived. Pulling the car into the driveway, a single porch light was glowing. Inside the house a light shone from the kitchen.

"We're here!" Sterling announced.

"Yes, we are. Thank you for everything. I will hope to hear from you soon," Rachel said. "Here, before you leave, let me give you my cell number if you hear anything."

She reached into her purse, pulled out a business card with her picture displayed, and smiled brightly. Underneath it was written: "Rachel Cooper, Golden View Real Estate, the answer to your housing needs."

"I didn't know you sold houses."

"Yes, no big," she responded after handing him the card.

"Make me a promise. If you hear anything, please call me."

"I will, I promise," Sterling responded.

He drove away, thinking about the two girls who were now strangers to him. They had been the focus of his life for so many months long ago.

Chapter 3

After Sterling saw Rachel safely to the door, he drove home thinking about Tom Taylor.

Pretty bold, Sterling thought. *To be that carefree, sending those flowers to Barbara's daughters, then immediately coming after their father. He doesn't seem a bit afraid of returning to prison for it. He is the only one with reason to target the family and practically signed a confession with those flowers.*

Analyzing what little he knew about the case, he soon arrived at his penthouse apartment in Manhattan. Unlocking his door, he slowly walked inside his residence. Immediately, he was encircled by his only companion in the world, Mr. Bigglesworth, his cat.

He picked up Mr. Bigglesworth and brought him into the kitchen, where he placed him on the cold, black granite countertop. He continued to caress the cat, who nudged him lovingly. Going to his leather address book, Sterling searched for a particular name. While he rummaged through the pages, his attention was diverted by his cat's attempts to shower him with attention. His curly tail would periodically dance across Sterling's face, prancing back and forth while purring softly.

Sterling turned to the starved-for-affection cat, chuckling as he murmured, "You poor thing. I left you alone for the entire afternoon."

Taking him up in his arms, he rubbed his head as he remembered the evening's events. As he thought about it, it should have been no real surprise that Mark or any other family members would have been taken. It had been almost twenty years since the "Bishop Curse" ended. Barbara, with a bit of help from Sterling and his friends, had lived free of Tom Taylor the entire time, thinking they were safe. Tobias, the ancient evil sorcerer who had possessed Tom and tried to sacrifice Melissa and Rachel to become immortal, had been defeated. No one had ever imagined that Tom would be released from prison.

As he pondered the problem, he glanced around his apartment, noticing for the first time in the shadows of the evening how cold and uninviting the modern flat was. The black leather sofa. The expensive art on the walls. The molded bronze statues of humanity reach up for deliverance. A lone, or perhaps lonely, place he had made for himself. Walking to the large picture window, he gazed into the evening sky. The stars twinkled like diamonds set against black sand on a lonesome beach.

Taking a seat in his favorite chair, he set Mr. Bigglesworth down on the plush carpet and temporarily closed his eyes. The vision of Tommy Taylor flashed in his thoughts. He remembered the abandoned hotel, the last time he saw the boy.

Barbara pleaded for him not to allow Tommy to touch the dagger or her daughter, Melissa, would die. It was then when he maneuvered to where Tommy was standing. Unconscious, Tommy fell to the ground with a single chop to his neck.

Yes, the family was saved from certain death. His role in the victorious battle amounted to a single chop to a kid's neck. It was not much of a performance, but each player had their assigned task. His role was not as glamorous as Stannis's, but it also hadn't cost him his life, as it had poor Rothay and Shakira who faced horrible deaths that day.

Shakira, he thought, *the woman was so full of life.* He had promised himself to visit her grave. Something to add to the bucket list that never seemed to empty. Where did the time go? What happened to those days when time seemed as endless as the sands upon a seashore? But now, sitting alone, all that remained were the sad memories.

Memories such as Barbara's smile gave his solitary, depressing place a new meaning. That event, so many years ago, seemed as if it had happened only yesterday.

The curse was ended. Everyone assumed their lives would go on as if nothing ever happened. But had they all been wrong? Had their lives returned to normal? Or had they just been in a holding pattern, waiting for the next act in the drama?

Could everyone who survived the deadly encounter with Tobias pick up the pieces and start fresh? What of me, the loner? What of my life? The fact that love's happiness has never found me. The loved ones that meant so much in my life have dissolved between my fingers as if their images were made of sand.

Somewhat disgusted with the idea of love itself, Sterling closed his eyes and relaxed. Now, here in his place of solitude, he wanted it all to go away. All his thoughts of the dead calling out to him to be saved or rescued. Here, alone, he wanted more; he needed more than playing the savior of the undead. No, enough. This burden. If he could, he'd give it all away, the expensive lifestyle and collections of wealth, to have one hour alone to be in love. Not just in love but connected with someone who shared his thoughts. The physical attractions were, at most, temporary. When a soulmate is revealed, that person can end your sentences, being on the same wavelength as you—able to communicate by not only sound and words but also thoughts. To have someone who knows what you are about to say and has already agreed with you.

All possible for everyone else but not for him. *No, he thought disgustedly, the great psychic detective couldn't even get a date. All this seems stupid, but who gives a damn?* Yes, he was having a pity party, and a damn good one.

As Sterling sat, feeling desperate and alone, many emotions came to the surface, but one question remained: Was he to be alone for the remainder of his life? He wondered if he would ever experience love on a scale that so many spoke of and enjoyed. This question was one he often asked himself and, having no resources to find his answer, began to ponder and imagine himself alone and old. Not just old but decrepit and dying in a lone bed in a hospice treatment facility with no one around.

This darkness felt more burdensome than at any other time in his life. Wrought with emotion, Sterling felt overwhelmed. He hadn't the energy or strength to fight this desperate loneliness. Then the unexpected happened. He began to weep. His human frailty could no longer be ignored. He had locked his true feelings tightly inside a protected vault all these years. The more he thought of the children he would never have, the deeper his depression grew. He wept bitterly, all his strength depleted. Sterling, a man who's nothing more than a mortal—all alone. On this lonely planet, all by himself, the sad reality that he was never loved by his mother and barely understood by his father crashed upon him.

Sterling slammed his fist into the hard floor. The pain of his actions was not sensed. Could it be? In this place of desperation, the one act he could invoke was to harm himself, something he had never done before. Looking up, he stared at the ceiling and considered God, the infinite creator of the world in which we live.

Sterling was not religious; he could never be regarded as the church-going type but had few options at the end of his rope. *There must be something to this God thing*, he thought. Why do people gather each Sunday to pay homage? Had he missed the bus entirely? Had he looked at life more indifferently than everyone else? He must know. He had to know! Above him, the high white ceiling but beyond, higher than the highest mountain, must be where God lived. Those lessons were taught to him in school when the bus would arrive on Fridays to educate children on who God was. He was no different; his happy bachelor uncle thought it best for the young Sterling to be educated in things religious and signed him up.

He actually enjoyed the teachings from the Bible. Significantly, the teacher seemed interested in Sterling's spiritual enlightenment. The nightmares, the damn visions of the dead speaking from beyond the grave, that world seemed to mix with his childhood and made him resist anything spiritual, even the God stuff. As a man, he was responsible for his decisions, of which the hardest to bear was living a life of solitude, alone.

Something—was there something wrong with him? A sin never confessed? A decision or lustful desires contrary to God's beliefs? Now, here and now, he would face his greatest fears and ask, yes, ask God for his help.

What is the human state, he wouldn't begin to guess, that kept him a prisoner from love, from her, whoever she was, this love of his life?

Wiping his tears, he was transfixed by staring at the ceiling to seek his answer. He started to pray, to seek God, but how? One thing he did remember from his religious teachings that the teacher always said was that God was a God of love. Somehow this made sense, a God of love; it was something he was looking for. Closing his eyes, Sterling began to pray. When he did, the reality of his broken heart was suddenly exposed. All his hurt and pain were made bare as if he was shown his deepest secrets from which he could no longer hide. In that place where his love should flourish, it seemed blocked by some darkness.

Surrendering everything to this maker of the universe, Sterling felt the blockage dissolve. As it did, his surroundings changed. He felt new freedom, and at first it felt scary and unsure. But then the strangest thing happened: The world around him changed, and he found himself in his favorite island setting. He often found himself here in his mind and always alone. This time, dressed in a bathing suit, he stood on a beach, his feet in the sand. Not far away the waves lapped the shore. Not far off children played and made sandcastles. Voices talked and laughed with one another.

A man was talking, saying something hard to make out. Turning to see who it was, he saw a waiter holding a platter of tropical drinks and ice cream cups. Next to him was a woman lying in a beach chair. As Sterling watched, the waiter handed the woman a glass.

He gave her a receipt to sign and said, "Ms. Cornwall, I hope you're enjoying your visit to St Thomas."

"Oh, indeed, we are, aren't we, darling?"

In utter shock and amazement, Sterling stared at the shapely legs and pink toenails.

"Children, hurry. Mommy has gotten you some ice cream!" Signing the small paper, the woman handed it back to the waiter and said, "Oh, by the way, my name is no longer Ms. Cornwall; it's Mrs. Sterling, thank you!"

Sterling gasped and froze in place. He didn't move for some time, stunned by the vision. As he attempted to focus on specific details of the beach scene and the woman, he heard a voice speaking his name as if it were in the room. As he opened his eyes to look about, a dark object appeared in a blur. Suddenly, a fist struck him across his jaw, sending him to the floor, and the room suddenly spun out of control.

The last thing he heard was a harsh voice laughing; it echoed as if from a long distance away. Then a voice said, "Sterling, you fool, would you think I would forget what you did that day? No, my friend, I'm leaving you a gift, something to remember me."

Sterling's eyes rolled up in his head as he collapsed, unconscious.

Chapter 4

MARK HARDING STRUGGLED to open his eyes. His head pounded badly. Blood dripping from the wound in his head had dried over his right eyelid, making it difficult to see. He tried to move his arms only to discover himself bound tightly, and as his awareness slowly returned, he realized his arms were tied over his head from the ceiling. He stood there with nothing on except his briefs. His shirt and pants had been removed. Even his shoes had been removed, the floor cold on his bare feet.

As he focused on the room, he noticed a large glass window on an opposite wall overlooking the ocean below. Rain splattered against it, cold and uninviting.

The room was decorated exquisitely with many chrome sculptures, several resembling dragons. There were pictures of demonic battles with mighty angels on the wall. Others depicted scenes of humans writhing in kettles of boiling oil as their bodies were cut asunder to be thrown to lizard-like animals. Carved ivory angelic creatures were making love to a mortal woman. An assortment of instruments of death hung on the walls, swords and battle axes coated with blood from the victims that suffered under their sharp edges. Other bronze works included dark satanic figures fighting angelic beings, and large paintings on the walls were of pentagrams and upside-down crosses.

The wall to his side held another window shaped like a dragon's eye that curved in an oval pattern. This entire wall was painted an off-green color, unlike the surrounding walls, which were a dark brown. Around the window large scales resembling the dragon's skin were set in the plaster.

Inside the dragon's eye was a large red ruby decorated in gold, supported by wires resembling blood vessels. Just below the eye was a white stand made of stone. Upon it lay an old book opened to a particular passage.

Mark shivered uncontrollably. This place was dedicated to pure evil. Whoever lived here devoted themselves to the worship of malevolent beings. It had been a long time since Mark had any involvement with the occult. Only one man, to his knowledge, took such pleasure in expressions of pure evil as this: Tom Taylor, the only male survivor of a cursed family. Tom, he knew, had recently been paroled from prison.

Mark remembered that day when the story splattered across the airways. Somehow the parole board concluded that Tom had served enough time for the pain he had caused and was no longer a threat to society. They released him back into the population. The effect on Mark's daughters was devastating. At least by that time Barbara's cancer had been so advanced that she had been unaware of Tom's release. Otherwise, Mark couldn't imagine what his wife would have done to remove the man who had helped to kidnap and tried to kill their daughters.

Tom had even given an interview with the news media after his release. It was some late-night host who only gave a damn about ratings, not the murderer he was talking about.

There, live on television, Tom Taylor appeared, now grown, explaining his virtuousness to the world. His father had manipulated him…he had only been a kid, a teenager…nothing that had happened had been his fault…he hadn't meant to start the fire that killed his siblings.

His attempts to express his innocence only brought a burning resentment that heightened Mark's anger. He practically threw the remote at the television when Tom said that all the charges of kidnapping and murder were false; they had been manufactured by the police and the Bishop-Harding family. He was simply an innocent man, unjustly incarcerated.

For weeks the paparazzi followed Tom's every move, the lavish dinners at restaurants and shopping sprees galore. It was as if Tom was a famous movie star. However, when it came to his victims, no one gave them a passing thought. It was Tom Taylor, the man of the hour.

Mark heard a commotion behind him and struggled to see what it was. He heard a door close, followed by footsteps in his direction. Suddenly, a young, pregnant Hispanic girl dressed in black quietly entered the room. She carried a black cloth object, which she gingerly placed on the white marble table. The cold granite piece resembled an altar, Mark realized. She began to untie the string that held the cloth together. Unrolling the item, Mark could see the contents inside, each tool some shiny stainless-steel cutting device that Mark was sure he would soon experience.

The girl looked up at him, her hair black as night. She wore dark mascara, and her face was painted around her eyes, hiding any sign of humanity. She smiled quickly, walked over, and sat in a chair against the wall. Crossing her legs, she waited.

Something outside the room caught his eye. Glancing toward the patio, he could see through the window; he noticed a large table. He recognized it. How could he not? It was the same table that Melissa had been tied to when Tom had wanted to sacrifice her. He remembered seeing it back at the abandoned resort when he came to pick up his family once his wife and Sterling had saved the day. The table looked new, recently polished, with ornately carved images on its legs. The mystical signs were carved deep into the stone surface. Now it sat alone on the patio as if still waiting for the taste of blood. Mark shivered again as he stared at it.

How long he waited, bound and staring at the silent girl and the stone altar, he did not know. Finally, another girl with bright red hair walked into the room. She went to stand under the dragon's eye and picked up the book, placing it down on the marble altar. Then she silently took a seat next to the other girl. This girl, too, was pregnant.

The door opened again, and a muscular young man in his twenties walked in. His skin was a bright white color. The color of his hair was white as snow, and his eyes glowed an eerie red. The albino carried a small black cauldron with red-hot burning embers inside. Taking the kettle, he sat it down on a metal stand next to the marble altar. Inside the bowl three branding irons stuck out; their ends glowed red-hot.

He sat down in a black leather chair beside the young woman. He removed large asbestos gloves and set them on a small coffee table before him. No one spoke; they looked like well-trained lap dogs. Each looked straight ahead, wearing a stupid, silly smile that Mark intensely disliked. The red-haired girl looked at Mark finally and smirked. She was missing a tooth. It had been knocked out in the struggle to take him as a prisoner.

Mark called them, "So tell me, when will my host arrive?" He got no response. It was as if they were all under some spell, lost in some optimistic vision Mark could not see.

The pounding in his head didn't cease. Now close to sixty years old, his arms tied above him soon ached to the point that they hurt worse than the bump on his head. He wished to be free from this horrible place. He knew that his echoing screams of pain would soon fill the space, wall to wall.

Suddenly, a man in his early forties appeared in the room, carrying scrolls of ancient paper under his arm. It had been many months since he had last seen Tom Taylor's face on the television, but he knew who it was.

"Are you comfortable?" Tom asked without emotion. Mark knew the game had now begun.

"I suppose I'm as comfortable as I can be. I see your pets are waiting to perform your commands, which ultimately will end in my demise."

"Oh, let's not get melodramatic over this. The part you played was more of an innocent bystander, not like that bitch of a wife of yours. What I hated most was what she did, which led to my being behind bars for all those years. Too bad she is rotting in the ground now, and I can't have my revenge, but I'll gladly use you instead," Tom boldly announced.

"Listen to me, boy, I'm not sure who you think you are, but you can just leave my innocent wife out of all of this," Mark demanded.

"Leave her out of this, you say?" Tom laughed. "You see, I already did all I could do to that poor woman. I'm the one responsible for her death and no other."

"You had nothing to do with Barbara getting cancer," Mark yelled. "That was just an act of God's will upon her life and nothing more, you sick-minded son of a bitch. It was in the cards she was dealt. Ovarian cancer was just something she meant to have; it certainly had nothing to do with you."

"You weak-minded old dog, that's where you're wrong; I had everything to do with it. Down to the very spell that created cancer, your wife died before her time." Tom laughed again, remembering his hand in Barbara's demise.

"Say whatever you need to convince yourself, boy, but let's get this over with; you're boring me to tears," Mark said, attempting to bring all the contempt he felt for this man into his voice.

"We shall see how bored you are a few minutes from now. You see, I have unique plans, not only for you but for your daughters as well. Please, do not think I have forgotten them for a moment. I will never forgive. Soon they will die, rotting in the ground just like your wife."

"Listen to me, loser, I'm not afraid of you or your little lap dogs."

"You talk a good game, my friend, but I can't help but see you trembling."

"No, I'm not trembling because I'm scared of you; no, you're mistaken. I'm trembling because of my low blood sugar, plus my muscles are not used to this sort of restraint."

"We'll soon see."

Looking around the room, Mark said, "I see you gathered some artifacts of that fateful event twenty years ago. I even noticed the sacrificial table, which your master tried to use to kill my daughter. You will undoubtedly use it in some sacrifice, of which I'm sure I'll play a part."

"Tobias was a fool. He had every opportunity to destroy your daughters but lacked the skill to control the gifts the dark lord gave him that day. Eventually, he was defeated. However, I have gained the favor of the dark lord, much greater than Tobias. He has granted me access to hidden powers that mortal men have only dreamt of obtaining. He has given me a new teacher named Drasidan, a demon with exceptional abilities."

"Whatever forces you have at your disposal, just know that, again, you will find yourself on the losing end."

"You think that someone will swoop in to rescue your worthless carcass? Look around the room; there's no one here to save you. My pets do my bidding; they obey without question. It is you who is on the short end. Today is the day you will die. The branding irons are red-hot, and the cutting tools are as sharp as razors."

Mark couldn't deny the fear he felt. He knew his life was over but was not looking forward to the torture he understood was ahead of him. He tried to disguise his feelings from this monster, however.

"Have you forgotten the friends my wife had made, who possess strength stronger than you? It shall not take them long before they come to my aid. Just like the miserable black wizard Tobias, you will perish. Do not think you will escape your punishment, no matter what you do to me!"

"Forgot, you say?" Tom yelled out in response, his

anger at the lack of fear this older man showed getting the better of him. "I'm the one who has been forgotten for years in that prison cell. I was neglected, pawned off, and abused by sick-minded people. I had been forgotten, left to die in the wretched hell that your family stuck me in. No, now society will pay the price for their forgetfulness."

"Listen to me, sicko. People like you are forgotten as much as a society can forget; only the memory of your horrid acts of murder remains a lesson to teach us that cruel monsters exist in this world."

"No, I will not be forgotten, but you will, old man. I promise you that the world will continue in its degradation, but your remains will be used to create something most precious. No memory of you or that bitch wife of yours will remain."

"Boy, if you continue calling my beloved wife that name, I will get free and kick your ass in front of your cronies."

Tom laughed aloud and picked up a dark iron thong. Scrutinizing it, he said, "Now, tell me, will anyone remember you twenty years from now? Especially since your family will all be dead. However, I have taken steps to ensure that my legacy survives for the millennium and beyond. But it's sad to say that the Bishops will be erased from existence. Enough of that; I don't want to spoil any of the fun I have in store for this world."

Addressing Aeneas, Tom's protégé, he said, "Bring me the ruby."

The young man left and returned with a large stone in hand a moment later. Presenting the precious gem to his master, he bowed respectfully, returned to the other side of the marble altar, and stood perfectly still.

Something strange happened as Tom held the precious stone and gazed into the reflected surface. A dark shadowy figure appeared from beneath the floor. The ghostly creature entered his body, causing him to have strange muscular convulsions.

He turned to Mark, a hauntingly sinister smile on his face. Still holding the red ruby, Tom's voice became a deep resounding echo. "Honoish, Zorro, Poppish, Din." Suddenly, a reddish light emitted from the ruby. The light grew wider.

Putting up a good fight, Mark struggled to get free, but the bindings around him kept him helplessly in place.

The reddish glow that spread out from the stone as Tom approached displayed unique cryptograms. Some looked like pentagrams, upside-down crosses, and faces of dragons. Various inscriptions were written in a strange language—all combined within the bright curtain.

Mark helplessly watched. As the reddish light penetrated his feet, he heard an ear-piercing scream as the reddish glow burnt into his flesh. The symbols were now shown as deep burn marks, several layers down into his tissue.

The pain continued until his entire body displayed burning symbols. As the pain became too great to bear, Mark passed out, only to be awakened again and again as the torture continued until at last, close to dying, Mark surrendered to the tortuous incantations.

Having finished with Mark's torment, the red ruby was taken away. Now something more horrible was soon to be experienced. Tom, chanting a spell, caused the red-hot coals inside the black cauldron to turn white-hot. Grasping one of the irons, Tom approached.

Staring intently at the metal poker, Mark saw its end had a pentagram design.

Seeing Mark's misery, Tom laughed and said, "Oh, but wait, we're not finished."

The torment continued as Tom buried the branding iron deeply into Mark's forehead. As he screamed out in agony, Tom laughed continuously as the aroma of burnt flesh filled the space.

Under the torturous pain, Mark was about to perish, hearing Tom's fading words to his followers, "Now the pig is prepped for slaughter. Retrieve the blades."

Why the hate toward him, Mark could never understand. Why had Tom Taylor had it out for him? Yes, he was the patriarch of the Harding family but nothing more. He wasn't a Bishop—he had only married someone with that last name.

His part in destroying this boy's wizard master had been nothing to speak of; no, he had nothing to do with this crazy magic stuff. He had never been confident that any of the black magic his wife and daughters described was true. He knew Tom believed it. He accepted that his family thought it. He was grateful for Sterling's help in returning his family to him, but a part of him had always believed it was sleight of hand, a show of intimidating his young, impressionable daughter.

Barbara had told him it was real. No, it couldn't have been confirmed. It was all true. A man turns into a dragon and fights a so-called sorcerer. Spidery creatures with sharp little pinchers tried to eat his daughters. He had convinced himself of that and had come to believe it after many years. But now he knew he had been wrong.

Barbara, his wife, was gone and buried. Mark would soon be joining her. But what would happen to him before the end? He could only imagine. Tom, this sick-minded puke, was determined to make him suffer, but he had never done a damn thing to Tom. Shit, he barely knew him except for what he'd read in the newspapers. Well, there was no time for pity.

Moments away from death's door, Mark was confident of his demise. Why now? How did he find himself about to die for the crime of marrying Barbara Bishop? Something that happened a lifetime ago, back in his past, when they first met at a rock music store. It was during the 1970s when the world was on edge, going crazy, much like today.

His mind could no longer stand the torture, and he drifted away, back in time to that day he had met Barbara. He saw himself hanging around with his best friend, Steve, listening to music being played on the loudspeakers overhead. Barbara walked inside the store, wearing an Indian-type wrap around her body. With her long, flowing blonde hair, he and his friend quickly noticed her. The question was always the same: Which one would pursue her if she was free?

A life lesson learned early: The woman always chooses who she wants to be with, no matter how much a man thinks differently. It was the same in this situation. Relaxed or acting cool was his trademark modus operandi. He ignored the beautiful blonde—or at least pretended that he did—as he and Steve continued discussing the future rock concert planned for the following week.

But he didn't ignore how she turned when leaving the record store. The second glance meant she was interested in one of them, although at the time neither could guess which.

Mark's vision of the past dissolved, and his

consciousness returned to the room where he was now trapped. The party of demented shits had just returned. The smiles plastered on their painted faces meant the show was drawing to a close. Too late now to reminisce or remember.

Tonight, ladies and gentlemen, I shall undoubtedly be cut asunder for my final performance as a man. He must be delirious, he thought. *How can I be making jokes to myself as I'm about to die?* Still, his inner voice continued. The instrument of his demise, held by little Tom Taylor, glistened in the light. Its saw-like teeth looked sharp and ready.

Mark suddenly noticed a dark shadow following Tom. Something was barely visible between the two stupid girls, but when he looked directly at it, there was nothing but absolute darkness. Tom appeared before Mark, holding his butchery instrument and wearing his sinister crooked smile. The ghostly apparition passed through his body and stopped inches away from Mark. As this demon creature surveyed Mark, eyeing carefully the deep burns marking his body, it spoke: "Well done, Taylor. I so enjoy seeing the sacrifice prepared properly for slaughter,"

"Do your worst, you sick-minded piece of shit. Whatever hole you crawled out from will not save you. For you see I have read and studied the Bible; I know how it ends. What does it matter what you do to me now? In the end when you are judged, this day will be remembered sometime in the future. Someone is keeping score; I'm certain of this."

"Oh, if that were true, but no, I'm afraid your hopes for the eternal are for nothing. Today your body will be sacrificed. But be of good cheer for it will mean that your screams will go on eternally, forever a prisoner of the dark lord."

"You keep thinking that, boy. Won't you be surprised?"

"Listen, you foolish mortal, you no longer speak to Tom Taylor. Do you not realize I have survived since the dawn of time? You have no hope of life to tell the tale. Now it all ends for you. Taylor, do your duty and deliver this fool to your lord."

"No, again, you're wrong. Death is only the beginning, not the end."

"Taylor, have you not the stomach for sacrifice?" The demon, for that is who it must be, Mark thought, snarled at Tom. And Mark realized that while Tom thought he was the master, he was wrong. This demon and the dark lord he spoke of would always rule Tom.

"End this man's life at once, end the misery in my aching ears from the sounds of his babblings, or else I'll do it for you," the demon cried.

Mark began to pray aloud. Not sure how to react as his victim prayed to God, Tom seemed uncertain as he stupidly held the weapon, not knowing what to do. The demon creature, realizing his protégé's hesitation, took possession of Tom's body, controlling him. The blade was raised high instantly and quickly came down in a brutal slashing motion. Blood splattered everywhere across the room, coating all in a deluge of red substance.

Memories of the life he once lived were quickly snuffed out, all forgotten in a single act of cruelty. The life of Mark Harding was over.

Chapter 5

ARRIVING AT THE SMALL CAFÉ, Sterling saw Rachel waiting for him at a table. She looked at him in surprise.

"Oh my god, Sterling, what happened to your lip?"

"Yes, my fat lip?" Sterling responded.

"Looks like someone hit you pretty hard."

"Yes, someone or something did, for sure."

Just then a waitress stepped up and took their drink orders. A moment later she returned and gave Sterling his tea and Rachel her coffee.

After she left them, Sterling looked at Rachel with concern and said, "Rachel, please listen to me for a moment. I haven't told anyone about what happened to me the other night, but now I feel compelled to do so."

"What do you mean?"

"After I dropped you off at your home, I returned to my apartment. No one was there except for my cat, Mr. Bigglesworth."

Rachel tried not to giggle at the thought of the dignified man in front of her with a cat named Mr. Bigglesworth.

"I got undressed and got comfortable for a quiet evening at home. I was ordered by your mother not to allow Tommy to touch the Jillian Dagger or else your sister would die. Well, the battle was fought to save you and your sister. I recalled that fateful day when Tommy was just a boy working for that wizard Tobias. I raced to where he was hiding, gave him a karaka chop on the neck, and sent him unconscious to the ground."

"I barely remember anything about that day," Rachel admitted.

"You are lucky. Truthfully, I would love to forget that day and everything associated with it but, unfortunately, I cannot. As I was saying the other night, as I sat there thinking about Tommy, suddenly, out of nowhere, I heard a man's voice call out my name. I looked about the room and saw a flash of light, and suddenly something resembling a human fist struck me across my jaw, knocking me to the floor, unconsciousness."

"What! Really, Sterling, that sounds too weird to be true."

"Rachel, you still have doubts after everything you've seen in the supernatural world?"

"I've grown up, Sterling. I have chosen to forget those things that happened to my family so long ago and wish to blot them from my memory."

"Well, I wish you a lot of luck in your endeavor," he said with a hint of sarcasm. *How could Barbara's daughter deny what had happened?* he thought. She had been an integral part of the whole affair. "However, the fact remains that your father has been taken, and it's obvious who's behind it."

"On that much we can agree. Tom Taylor, that bastard," Rachel muttered under her breath.

"I cannot imagine anyone else. It's Tom Taylor, I'm sure of it."

"Sterling, it's been almost two weeks, and still, the police have not found my father. Each day leaves me desperate and believing he'll never be found." A pause of silence, then Rachel began to cry.

Sterling reached over to hold her hand as the pinned-up emotions erupted, refusing to be contained any longer.

After several moments Rachel wiped her eyes and said, "Did I ever tell you that Tommy wrote my sister, Melissa?"

"No. Really, why?"

"Well, it seems he had a moment of weakness and wanted to apologize for the heartache he caused my family. However, he never got any response from either my sister or me. No, as far as we were concerned he could rot behind bars."

"I knew he would be released from prison one day; I saw it in a premonition," Sterling announced.

"You did? Then please tell me why you didn't feel the need to warn any of us."

"I couldn't be sure that it was a real threat. After all, Tom had been locked away behind bars and wasn't to be released back into society again. And what good would it have done you? It would have brought you all stress and fear for years before it happened."

"I suspect everyone was wrong in their estimations. Already I see acts of his cruelty and what he's done to you," Rachel declared.

Taking a sip of her coffee, Rachel sat down her cup, looked at Sterling, and announced, "Sterling, I haven't said anything to my family, but I know about the affair between you and my mother."

Sterling sipped his tea nervously, glancing at the young woman eyeing him. After careful consideration he responded. "Please listen to me; those were difficult times in my life and your mother's. She was unhappy; she and your father had separated so we grew closer than we should have. After a short time she saw the futility in our relationship and returned home to be with your father, Mark."

Picking up her cup of coffee, Rachel tasted it and said, "She loved you, you know."

"I loved her as well, but those days are gone forever, and now there's a more pressing matter to contend with."

"My father's whereabouts, I know, but where to look is the question."

"When it comes to finding your father, I doubt conventional methods will help. No, not when it comes to the supernatural."

"What about your friend, that powerful sorcerer named Stannis?"

"Stannis? I haven't heard from him in a long time— years, in fact. I have tried to reach out many times, both through the natural world and the supernatural. Several years after the incident with Tobias, he fell off the radar. We used to talk regularly. We collaborated on a few cases together, but over the past years he has grown distant. I respected his decision," Sterling explained.

"Well, we must do something! Tommy Taylor, I believe, is out to kill us all. I see what fools we were in believing he could never harm us again." Rachel started to cry.

"Rachel, please listen to me. We can win this fight. It would help if you kept the faith; it's all we have," Sterling said, grabbing her gently by the arm.

"Oh, sure, I know that. But truthfully, I've accepted that my father is possibly dead, and we could be next to die."

"Why on earth would you say that?"

"Listen to me. Have you been able to feel Tom's

presence?" Rachel asked.

"Well, the truth is I haven't tried."

"I haven't felt his presence; it's as though he has left this world, and we're all waiting in line for our turn to ride the 'death rollercoaster' at this loathsome circus."

"Sometimes it feels that way, I know. But if we just drop to our knees and allow evil to have its way, there will be no future for our children or us," Sterling explained.

"Our children, the next generations that are to follow our paths. What adversities will they face in their lives one can only imagine."

"You're right; there will be no future for our descendants if evil continues so we must not give up hope."

Looking at her watch, Rachel announced, "The kids will be leaving school soon, and I have to run. I still haven't heard anything from the police or Jacob. I was hopeful that if we met today you would at least offer me a ray of hope. But you never said a word yet about your ability to feel my father's life source."

"Okay, listen, I haven't searched for your father mentally because of the connection he might have with Tom Taylor. I admit I'm not sure I'm strong enough to go up against him alone. But when I find Stannis, I will do everything possible to find your father. You have my word."

"I believe you."

"This afternoon I'm going to travel to where Stannis once lived and see if I can find out what happened to him. We need his help; he's the only one powerful enough to fight Tom Taylor."

"Alright, whatever you say. I have to get going. If

any news, call me immediately."

"I will. I promise you."

"Look, there's something I've always wanted to ask you."

"Yes, what is it?"

"Sterling, what does it mean? My sister and I have always wanted to ask you, but it seems there has never been the proper time. Could you, I mean, are you willing to tell me? I know with everything going on why ask, right? I don't know; maybe it's just my way of diverting myself from the sad reality that my father is dead at that man's hands. Again, we just wanted to know." Rachel began crying again, overwhelmed with heartfelt emotions.

Sterling took hold of Rachel's arms, gripping her tightly. "Sebastian Martin. That's my true name; your mother knew it but kept my secret. The name Sterling, Sterling Silver, invokes purity so I chose the name, wanting to be pure, apart from evil!"

"Yes, but doesn't evil find us in the end, no matter how far we run? Look, it found my father, right?"

"I suppose."

"Why did you tell me your name now?"

"I suppose I just wanted some other person in the world to know the real me," Sterling said with a sad smile.

"I understand. Look, Sterling, your secret is safe with me although, if it is alright with you, I will probably share it with my sister. Besides, no one else needs to know; it's doubtful they would understand, especially this young generation. Look, I've got to leave; I'm late. Thank you, Sterling."

"For what? I haven't really done anything."

"I know, but being here with us girls seems right as

if Mother would have wanted it that way. As weird as it sounds, if things were different, you could have been our stepfather. Who knows?"

"Yes, who knows? Life, what can we say?"

"Goodbye." Placing a kiss on his cheek, Rachel hurried out the door, not looking back.

Watching Rachel leave, Sterling gave a final wave as she left the café. Sitting alone, he wished he could do more to help the Bishop family. But by himself, he wasn't powerful enough. A sad reality, indeed. In truth, he knew of only one person equipped to battle such evil forces: Stannis himself. Mark's essence seemed to have vanished. Perhaps his life was already ended, tortured to death at the hands of Tom, although he hadn't wanted to admit this to Rachel, who seemed to have already lost hope that her father was alive.

Looking at his watch, Sterling saw it was just past one o'clock that afternoon. He had plenty of time to drive upstate to explore Stannis's old digs. He quickly called over the waitress and paid the bill.

Chapter 6

Leaving the café, he got into his black Porsche and drove away from White Plains toward the little town of Sleepy Hollow, nestled along the Hudson River. The busy highway soon thinned out, and only a few cars were left on the road, allowing him time to revisit the past.

Thinking about the past twenty years was not a pleasurable experience, especially when it came to remembering Barbara Bishop Harding. The woman had stolen his heart. Yes, the events that involved her family were unique, and no one would have believed that such things still existed in the hidden shadows of the modern world, but they did. Even today the forces of good and evil rage against each other.

The miles passed slowly, coupled with Barbara's memory, which made him feel somewhat hopeless. Feelings of loss and sadness invaded his thoughts. Barbara's smile and laughter were now passing memories. He had been there when she took her final breath. The doctors told the family that she still had a few days to live, and they went home to rest that night. But somehow he knew. His spiritual connection to Barbara told him she wouldn't last until morning, and he had returned to the hospital.

Death had arrived too quickly for him, even though

Barbara had worn a contented expression. She had squeezed his hand. Then, after a final gasp of her lungs, she was gone. The alarms rang out at the nurse's station, and it was time to leave. Nothing more could be done. That night he mourned her loss in private. As he remembered her death and the feeling of loss, a tear formed and dropped down his face. *Love is such a simple word with such a powerful meaning.*

His turn-off appeared, and he followed a small group of cars exiting the freeway. He turned right at the signal, headed in the northerly direction, and followed the Hudson River; it had been some years since he last traveled this road. It was the only way to reach Stannis's dwelling. The highway continued over small hills decorated with lush trees and small farms. The road became busy as it weaved in and out of miniature metropolises.

He saw a highway sign that read: "Sleepy Hollow Next Three Exits." Sterling took the last one and came to a stop sign. Turning right, he followed the road through the small city of Tarrytown until he arrived at River Street. There he tried to find a parking space in the busy center. Suddenly, a car's brake lights lit up, and a vehicle pulled out. Pulling behind it, he maneuvered his vehicle's tires tightly against the curb.

As he exited, a nearby restaurant's kitchen sent a pleasant aroma into the street—he would have to visit before he returned home. Walking across the busy street, he reached the pier overlooking the Hudson River and stopped, shocked. Stannis's ship was moored where it had always been, but now it was half-sunken, with water entering the fourth deck. Seagulls sat upon the upper decks, and the ship's bridge had its windows knocked out. It looked utterly ruined. Sterling stared at the disaster.

Stannis must be dead, he thought, *otherwise, why would his prized ship be lying in such devastation?* The sight was sad to look upon and seemed to fit his mood. He had memories of Barbara being here with him. It seemed fitting that the ship was gone, just as she was. His thoughts wandered to what Rachel had said: Why would Barbara even tell her such personal information?

He sighed in despair. His last hope for help in finding Mark was gone. All the players in the previous game of life and death seemed to have left the table. Who else could he consult? Walking over to the pier's edge, he placed his foot on the railing and gazed down into the murky water, defeated. Could he still rely on his powers of observation? His innate knowledge of people? His psychic connections to the spirit word? No, his abilities seemed to fade with the twilight of the ending day.

As he stared into the salty water, he noticed an opening below. It had been Stannis's front door, the main entrance to his home. He remembered the once elaborate entrance leading to the boat's interior. There were ferns, ceramic pots, ornate carpets, and marble floors decorating the foyer. Inside the room opened to a vast, even more, elaborate area several stories high. How had it all fit inside this small ship? Ah, that was Stannis's secret. All that was now erased and forgotten in the cloudy waters, leaving Sterling empty and sad. Stannis was truly gone.

Sterling reached out and took ahold of the railing. A vision invaded his senses, and he experienced a magical presence. As he imagined the boat before, sometime in the past, he traveled back to where the monumental event that destroyed this ship had occurred.

In his mind he traveled back several weeks. It was late at night, and the sleepy town seemed deserted. Black clouds surrounded the pier and the entire ship. A man dressed in a long, black, hooded outer garment that covered his whole body stood upon the dock, holding a book in his hands. He was confronted by Stannis, who appeared from the bowels of his ship wearing a long white gown and a black belt wrapped around his big frame. Noticing the unwanted intruder, Stannis waved his hands in a circular motion and called out in a language unknown to Sterling. As his magic ended, the black shadows cleared, exposing the man to the dim light from the pier.

The enchantment had only slowed the man's intent, however. He, in turn, conjured a spell. A ball of flames erupted and rushed against Stannis and his ship with a loud boom as if a tidal wave had struck it. The vessel rocked side to side, tearing at its mooring lines. In response, Stannis lifted his arms above his head while yelling a different enchantment, and then, with all his might, he clapped his hands together. A bubble surrounded the other wizard; it continued to grow in size. It was translucent and glowed with magical energy against the darkened night sky.

Despite imprisonment inside the bubble, the wizard performed another enchantment, and a dark red dome grew from the book. It glowed as it met with Stannis's orb, and a dazzling array of sparks shot upward into the night sky. Unfortunately, the powerful magic of two great wizards were too much for the small space to encompass. A lightning bolt erupted between the two opposing forces, and an explosion of bright light vaporized both bubbles, sending the two men back to the ground.

Not wasting a moment, Stannis jumped to his feet and performed another spell. The ground underneath the other wizard became like quicksand, and he began to sink into the pier's pilings. Barely able to grip his book, he fell backward, struggling to maintain his balance and free himself. The more he struggled to escape, the faster he fell into black emptiness.

Stannis had the upper hand. He approached the man, intent on destroying the invader, when the dark wizard reached inside his cloak. He pulled out a red stone, lifted it, and a dark shadow appeared and entered him. He struck the book's cover, and a glowing red ring appeared near the wizard's feet. It narrowed and turned into a cone-like object that pierced the depths of the quicksand, dissolving it and freeing him. The conjurer disappeared in the reddish glow.

Stannis sagged to the ground, exhausted. As Sterling watched, the other wizard returned to view, focusing the stone's powers on Stannis. With a mighty swipe from his hands, the red light beam narrowed into a tubular ray directed toward his adversary.

Trying to avoid certain death, Stannis, with difficulty, reached inside a pouch that hung from his belt and removed an object that Sterling had seen before during a previous battle against evil: the Dragon's tooth, the most potent weapon Stannis had in his arsenal.

Stannis displayed his weapon, but just as he was about to ignite the fiery beam, the dark wizard shouted another incantation. Smoke rings rose from his book and shot across the sky, locking around Stannis's hands as if they were handcuffs and preventing him from igniting the dragon's power.

The dark sorcerer stepped close, speaking another charm from his book and holding his hands. His book of magic rose upward, levitating in space. Then it closed, and a loud explosion erupted like a storm approaching. The wizard repeatedly struck the book as beams of red, purple, and orange light exploded into sharp shards of light rays that hit Stannis in his chest.

The relentless assault drained Stannis of his strength. He could no longer maintain his illusions, not even his prized ship, which suddenly looked like nothing but a rusting hunk of metal.

Collapsing to the ground, Stannis lay there, knowing he was beaten. He could no longer fight off the evil power. He gasped for breath; he had all but given up the fight. He stared at his opponent with vile hatred. The dark wizard removed the hood. Sterling knew that face: Tom Taylor.

In disbelief, Sterling watched as Tom approached his fallen foe. Without speaking, he slammed his black book into Stannis's chest. A crashing boom rocked the nearby community, breaking lights and windows from the nearby stores and houses as if an explosion had occurred.

Stannis grabbed hold of his chest and gripped it tightly. The mooring lines behind him began to snap as his proud ship sank from a large, gaping hole in her port side. Stannis was alive. Sterling knew that because of the talisman he wore around his neck for protection. It was the only flicker of light that was visible. Without it, Stannis would have been obliterated in the fight.

Having defeated his enemy, Tom turned and disappeared in a dark cloud, returning to the hell where he belonged. Sterling continued watching a small scattering of townspeople come out of their houses to investigate the loud explosions. A woman from a nearby apartment suddenly saw Stannis lying unconscious on the pier. Racing to his side, she examined, then cried out for someone to call an ambulance.

The vision faded, leaving Sterling in awe of what he had witnessed. He now knew what had happened to the once powerful sorcerer: Stannis was defeated and lost. Tom Taylor had a powerful ally if he could defeat Stannis. Turning from the wreck, Sterling walked back to his car. Question after question invaded his thoughts. *What chance do we have to defeat Tom now? He is ill-equipped to fight enchanted battles of every kind. Is anyone else powerful enough to help me find Mark?*

Turning to leave, he walked across the street and approached his car. Near the restaurant a young man handed Sterling a flyer, then he continued down the sidewalk.

"Support our cause and scrap the rusty old vessel," shouted the young man. He stopped a small group of older people and eagerly handed each one a leaflet.

Sterling began to read the colorful paper printed with an image of Stannis's half-sunken ship and in bold letters: "Help Clean Our Town! Remove the Eyesore Ship!" Sponsored by the Tarrytown Beautification Project, it stated there would be a meeting at the high school gymnasium tonight at seven p.m.

Hmm, I might want to attend this meeting. Sterling decided to call the young man back.

"Hey, excuse me. Can you tell me who is behind this beautification project?" Sterling asked.

"All I know, man, is some guy who has invested a lot of money in the town has been complaining about that old wreck and wants it removed."

"Tell me, what happened to the original owner?"

Looking around for anyone listening, the young man leaned closer and whispered, "Well, I heard that

Aurelia Sabine, who lived across the street from the junky boat, witnessed some strange goings-on near the pier. She was the one that found the ship's owner unconscious. By the time the paramedics arrived, the owner had suffered a heart attack. They didn't expect him to live through the night."

"Aurelia Sabine, hm?" Sterling responded with raised eyebrows.

"Yep, Old Aurelia Sabine."

"So tell me, is she still living in the apartment?"

"Well, you know how it is, sir. My memory isn't what it used to be and all," the young man responded with a sheepish grin.

Reaching into his pocket, Sterling withdrew twenty bucks and handed it to the guy, "Tell me, how's your memory now?"

"Fine, just fine, thank you. Yes, Old Aurelia Sabine, what happened to the old gal is a shame. She died, you know! The good news is her granddaughter, Alexandra, still lives in that old apartment and refuses to leave, even though it's crumbling around her. Sorry, that's all I know." He turned and walked away.

He only took a few steps when Sterling announced, "If I were you, I wouldn't take any boat rides in the future; it might turn out to be fatal."

The guy stopped, turned around, and asked, "What`s that supposed to mean?"

Sterling smiled and said, "Sorry, that's all I know."

Then Sterling turned and walked into the restaurant. Inside delicious aromas filled his senses. Hanging on one wall were several prized fish. On the others hung old decorative fishing nets and floating buoys. Black and white photos of old local fishermen were scattered throughout. The outside sign declared the eatery's name as The Fisherman's Wharf. Not very original, but Sterling hoped the food was as tasty as it smelled. He eyed the establishment's interior while waiting by the counter to be seated.

Soon a waitress appeared. She grabbed a menu and asked, "Are you dining alone, sir?"

"Yes, it's just me."

"Please follow me, sir, this way."

Following the woman to an empty booth, Sterling scooted in and glanced out the window. The young man handing out the flyers was still standing on the sidewalk. He hadn't moved since Sterling gave his warning. Smiling at the man, Sterling turned his attention to the menu as the waitress appeared and asked for his order.

As he looked over the menu, he heard footsteps approaching. He glanced up and saw the young man.

Tossing the twenty on the table, the man said, "Here, buddy, here's your twenty back. I don't need it or a curse upon my head. You keep it."

"What? You have it all wrong, pal! I could have saved your life."

"What do you mean, save my life?"

"A word of warning is sometimes all it takes to make someone change their direction in life. A simple nudge, if you will. Hey, I've never eaten here before. You're a local. tell me, what do you recommend?"

Sitting at the booth, the stranger announced, "I'd stay away from the clam chowder, but the cod is always a fan favorite—order the fish and chips."

Turning around, he waved the waitress over, then sat opposite Sterling. When she arrived, he said, "Hey, sis, be a sweetie, will you, and bring me a beer."

Then, picking up the twenty from the table, he asked, "You don't mind, do you?"

"No, apparently not," Sterling said, amused by the young man.

"How about you, sir? Would you like something to drink?"

"Yeah, you know what, a beer sounds good. Bring us two."

As the waitress walked away, the young man stuck out his hand. "Let me introduce myself. My name is Mickey."

"How do you do, Mickey? My name is Sterling."

"Sterling, where have I heard that name before? Anywho, what you said earlier, how could you—Wait, now I remember. Wasn't there something that happened years ago involving a missing girl? Yes, that's it, Sterling. It's a name you don't hear that often."

Just then the waitress reappeared, carrying two beers and frosted glasses. Setting them down, she looked at her brother. "Mickey, I thought you were supposed to be working today."

"Yeah, I was. Did I tell you that I met the most interesting fellow on the way to the town square?"

"Who is that, Mickey?"

"Ever heard of a guy named Sterling? No? Well, now you have. Let me introduce you to Sterling."

"How do you, Sterling? Do you want to hear about today's specials?"

"According to Mickey, I'm to shy away from the chowder. Please just give me the fish and chips."

"Fish and chips, you got it. What about you, brother?"

"Hey, that sounds good to me, too."

"Hey, you still owe me from the last time you ate here, brother!"

"I'm good for it, sis. Just use what's left of the

twenty, and don't forget to give yourself a good tip."

Shaking her head in disgust, the waitress left the table.

"So, Sterling, I get it now when you told me about not taking any boat rides. Sure, I get that. But how do you know?"

"Sometimes my abilities ring true simply by closing my eyes to all outside influences. At other times emotions trigger my abilities. You, Mickey, pissed me off. Your little game of getting twenty bucks from me was disappointing."

"I realize that now. And I would like to apologize. Things haven't been as good as I would like lately. I've been out of work for months, and money is tight. You heard my sister; I can't afford to pay her for my meals. Seeing you drive up in that expensive car, I thought, 'What the heck, I'll try it.' I was hoping for a fifty!"

The young man had charmed Sterling with his honesty. They both broke out into laughter.

Their food arrived, and Sterling listened as Mickey chatted about the town. When they finished Sterling handed Mickey a fifty.

"Here, this might give you a reason to stop bumming money from your sister for a couple of days at least. Mickey, I'm picking up on something about you. I cannot be sure, but for whatever it means to you, go out and buy a lotto ticket. I think your luck is about to change."

"No shit; I will. I promise. Peace, brother."

With that they parted ways. Looking at his watch, Sterling had an appointment with the Tarrytown Beautification Project at the high school gymnasium and didn't want to be late.

Chapter 7

A WEEK HAD PASSED SINCE the disappearance of their father. The police hadn't found any clues; he seemed to have disappeared entirely. Melissa was at her wit's end. After reaching out to everyone they knew, her sister, Rachel, had agreed to meet with Sterling earlier in the week. Perhaps he could shine some light on their father's abduction. Lord knew the police had done all they could, with little to show for their efforts.

Melissa knew the hope of finding their father alive was dwindling. Tom Taylor had been questioned briefly, but that was all. He was free to come and go at will, without any repercussions. Yes, he was a person of interest in the case involving her father's kidnapping but nothing else. *He's living the good life while Rachel and I worry whenever the phone rings.*

It was upsetting that Tom was permitted to exist with no one knowing his whereabouts. However, if she had known where the man lived, she would have appeared at his door to demand her father's freedom. She knew without any doubt that the bastard had taken Mark. It was him and no one else.

But despite her father's disappearance, life continued, especially the need for food. One day she returned from grocery shopping and pulled her minivan into her garage. She walked back and forth to the car, carrying in her groceries. A messenger van came to a squeaky stop just before her home, and out rushed a delivery man who ran up the driveway and handed her a heavy box.

"Good afternoon, ma'am. I have a package for you. I need your signature here on this receipt."

"What is it?" Melissa curiously asked.

Looking down at the package, the man explained, "I'm not sure but, from what I can tell, it must be important. The sender overnighted it to you from the office of studies of ancient archaeology, associated with Monarch Hill University, Pittsburgh, Pennsylvania."

Melissa realized the package must come from Professor Etheridge, but she hadn't spoken to the man in years. Why on earth would he be sending her something now?

Professor Etheridge was one of the group of magicians and sorcerers Sterling had called together to defeat Tobias when she was captured. She hadn't seen or heard from him since that day.

Melissa hurried into the house, carrying the heavy package. She noticed the different labels that decorated the exterior of the box. One read: "Overnight Shipment." She stood back and examined it. It must weigh close to forty pounds. She sighed in relief as she set the heavy box on the dining table without dropping it.

The securely built box had several bolts that held steel plates in place—a metal band wrapped around the exterior. The heads of the pin were rounded with a strange design in the center, making it impossible to remove them without using a specialized tool.

Unfortunately, now was not the time to investigate the box. Melissa had to finish bringing in the groceries.

Already close to two o'clock in the afternoon, her sons would be getting out of wrestling practice. She lifted the box again, took it to the garage, and carefully set it on Dan's workbench. Then she put the meat and frozen items in the refrigerator. She looked at the time and hurried to pick up her sons.

The rest of the afternoon was hectic, filled with picking up Dan's clothes from the cleaners, a meeting with the wrestling coach, and later a dentist appointment for the boys. By the time Melissa arrived home, she was exhausted. Taking some chicken from the refrigerator, she deposited it in a pot with water and set the burner on high. A few minutes later the chicken was partially cooked. She coated the pieces with barbeque sauce and returned them to the refrigerator. The potatoes and green vegetables would be added separately. Dinner would be ready within the hour, just as Dan arrived home from the office.

After dinner her son Mark took out the trash. He noticed the strange box sitting on his father's workbench. When he walked back inside the house, he approached his mother.

"Hey, Mom, what's that strange-looking box on Dad's workbench?"

Dan, who had just gotten home, looked up from setting the dining table. "What strange box?"

"It just arrived today. Do you remember me telling you about a man named Professor Etheridge?" Melissa said.

"Sure, I guess. What about him?"

"Well, the box was from Monarch Hill University, where he once worked. No one has seen or heard from the man in years. And, to tell you the truth, I'm not sure he is still alive."

"Okay," Dan responded. "Perhaps I should look at this mysterious box."

"I wish you could, but I think it might be more difficult than you can imagine."

"Why do you say that?"

"It looks like it's made from weird-looking wood, secured by steel bands. The bolts have odd-looking centers. Opening them will take a special tool, and I'm guessing we don't have one."

"Now you have my curiosity piqued. You said it's on my workbench out in the garage? Let's go investigate."

Dan walked out into the garage with the entire family following. He flicked on his fluorescent lights. Before them sat the curious-looking box.

Taking a moment to examine the exterior, Dan stepped backward and announced, "I'm not sure what's inside. But one thing I do know: That box is made from the hardest wood known to man. It's called Australian Buloke, and it's expensive stuff!

"Back in college when I was studying to become an architect, we had to learn about different types of trees, including which trees were the strongest to use for the building projects you were designing. I found this tree particularly fascinating regarding expansion and stress factors for construction."

A puzzled Melissa turned to Dan and asked, "Why on earth would someone need to make such an object? What's inside that is so valuable?"

Dan looked back at his wife and said, "You got me."

"Well, it's definitely not something from Walmart. That much I know," Melissa announced.

Dan then took the box from the bench and held it

aloft while examining it closely, then he set it back down.

"I see what you mean about the fasteners holding it together. You cannot get those loose unless you want to destroy the contents. I suggest you contact Monarch Hill University to see if the guy you mentioned is still working there. Maybe you'll get lucky, and the guy can tell you how to open the damn thing."

"Sure, I'll call tomorrow."

"Well, listen, I have a project to complete for a board meeting tomorrow. I say forget about it for now; we'll deal with it when I get home tomorrow night. On second thought, we should lock it up in my gun safe if it's valuable."

"That's a great idea, honey," said Melissa.

Turning back around, Melissa told her kids, "Listen, boys, I believe you have homework so get to it."

"Sure, Mom," said her sons with disappointment.

The boys returned to the house, disappearing upstairs. Dan walked over to the adjacent wall to where his safe was located, punched in the password, pulled the heavy door open, and began moving ammo boxes. A few minutes late, he lifted the heavy object inside. Dan said goodnight to his wife, vanished into his office, and closed the door.

The following day while she was alone doing laundry, another messenger arrived with a small manila folder. This time unhindered, she opened the package. It, too, was from Monarch Hill University. Staring at the object in her hands, it looked bizarre. The tool was about six inches long and had a strange design on one end and a socket head on the other. Instantly, she realized it must be the needed part to open the mysterious box.

Finally, she thought. *Now perhaps I can see what treasure is inside that box.*

She walked out to where the gun safe was located and punched in the code. Taking hold of the metal wheel, she turned it counterclockwise and pulled the heavy door open. The green light lit, and the locks disengaged.

After she lifted the box from the safe, she took it to Dan's workbench and set it down with a thud. Reaching upward, she pulled the string on the overhead light. The fluorescent bulbs began to flicker and hum, and a moment later a bright light appeared.

Anxious to discover what was inside, she went to Dan's rollaway desk and opened a series of metal drawers until she found a three-eighths-inch drive ratchet. She snapped the widget into place. She matched the tool's design to the bolt head and removed all the box's securities. It took some time to remove each fastener, but after about twenty minutes the last pin was free. Lifting the clasp connected to the steel rod, she pushed open the lid to look inside.

What she saw was a surprise even to her. The interior walls of the box were lined with lead, including the top and bottom. A velvet cloth covered an object. Lifting it free, she found a note addressed to her underneath. She ripped open the delicate paper to read the letter.

Dear Melissa,

I'm so sorry to hear about your father. I want to offer my deepest sympathies. Our friend Sterling had informed me. Assuredly, I believe evil forces at work are menacing in nature.

When I heard your family was in trouble, I

immediately knew what to do. That is why I have sent you a weapon that will aid you. This item will be familiar to you in many ways. I believe in your hands wielding such a weapon will have consequences that evil cannot fight.

I've included a brief history of what's inside. Keep this safe; tell no one what you carry in your arsenal.

Professor Etheridge.

Again looking into the box, she removed another velvet cloth. Underneath sat an old-looking parchment, rolled up and held together by silken cloth. Next to it was a jeweled gold box. She took the old parchment and untied the knot. She unfolded it and quickly scanned the document. It was written in Latin. Thank goodness she had studied Latin in college. She lifted the parchment to the light to read it.

The Jillian Dagger: Instrument of death and revenge

Queen Jillian had come from a land far away. She'd only agreed to marry the conquering king after he threatened to murder her entire family. After King Osborn saw how lovely she was, he couldn't resist giving her his heart, including everything he possessed; he took her that afternoon to be his.

Unfortunately, marriage to Osborn meant nothing to her except an escape from the executioner's ax. Now that her family's lives were spared, the resentment on their faces was apparent at the wedding. That night should have told the king something was amiss when Jillian, his young bride, cringed at his flabby, old naked body, but he was too much in love to see the truth.

It was a tale as old as time. Unfortunately, so was the outcome. One day, while the king was away on a hunting trip, Jillian strolled inside the rose garden, feeling lost. As she miserably walked about, she heard a young man talking to someone on the other side of a stone wall. She drew closer to listen to what he was saying.

"Squirrel, you should talk now. I will happily listen to what you say if you do."

She peeked around the wall. There she saw a handsome young man standing next to a tree, dressed all in black with white stars sewn on his cloak. He was attempting to cast a spell, saying words in Latin that he mispronounced. Obviously, he was an apprentice to a great wizard.

The young man turned to see Queen Jillian staring at him. She had the face of an angel, with long blonde hair flowing past her shoulders and blue eyes that he could not resist. Instantly, the young apprentice, Markus, was taken by her beauty. She couldn't help but giggle at the sight of him.

Their love for one another grew. The affair they shared was kept secret—or so they thought. It was noticed by those who were loyal to the king. The king was hunting with court members when he overheard two squires joking about the queen.

"Throughout the night, making love to the queen, only to be awakened by such a fright. Young Markus's head gets stuck on a pike."

Suspecting the worst, the king raced back to

the castle, where he discovered the lovers on the spot where he had proposed marriage. The king was furious. He instantly imprisoned the queen in his dungeon. Her lover faced a crueler fate: He was immediately castrated and forced to work in the brothels. Sadly, he could only listen to the harlots' moans of pleasure, knowing that he would never again be capable of satisfying a woman.

Out of desperation, his torment lasted only briefly; he hung himself near where the queen was a prisoner. When the king learned what he had done, he ordered Markus's body to be suspended from the north gate, where the queen was forced to look upon it daily until there was nothing left of it but rotting flesh and bones.

The king's fury didn't end there. Forgetting his promise to the queen to save her father's kingdom, he returned with his army to slay her father, mother, and every man, woman, and child in the kingdom, preventing future generations from ever being born.

Now destitute, the queen waited for death, praying it would soon find her. Instead, Markus's teacher visited her. Disguised as a priest, he could see the queen daily.

They plotted for a way to gain back the king's favor, guaranteeing her freedom. But the truth was that she wasn't interested in escaping; she had plans for revenge.

The black wizard warned her not to take revenge upon the king. He explained that there was no way to escape the consequences of such a decision, but she refused to listen. So on one such visit, he returned with the ingredients required to destroy the king.

Love, the ultimate potion, was more potent than any other spell. The wizard knew of a particular enchantment: a love potion of forgetfulness and longing. When the wizard mixed the concoction, he informed the queen that she was to bathe her naked body in its ingredients, allowing the mixture to sink deeply into her skin.

Afterward she wrote a letter to the king, pledging her undying love. When the king saw the message, at first he ignored it. But when he looked at the scroll's brightly colored red ribbon, he was curious. He unrolled the parchment, and the queen's fragrance filled his nostrils. The effect was instantaneous; he immediately felt light-headed, like he had drunk too much wine.

The spell had done its work: The king forgot about the deceit. Unfortunately for him, the queen hadn't forgotten. The king ordered the queen to be brought to his chamber at once. A short time later he looked upon her beauty as if seeing her for the first time. Under the spell's effect, the King ripped her clothing from her body and made love to her until the morning hours.

He couldn't get enough of her essence and was never satisfied until exhaustion overtook him, and he fell asleep. While he lay there peacefully, Jillian stared down at him with loathing. The wizard had warned her that killing a king was not easy; if she faltered, then powers unknown that protected monarchs and royals could be released to destroy her.

She looked at the king sprawled on his back and calmly removed her purse, which she had brought with her containing a gift from the dark wizard. Reaching inside the bag, she felt the sharp object poking her finger. Immediately, she began bleeding. Ignoring the dripping blood, she pulled the dagger free.

Filled with disdain, the queen returned to the bed and crawled atop the king. She raised the dagger. Repeating words from a spell the wizard had taught her, she gripped the handle tightly and shouted, "This is for Markus and my family, you heartless, pathetic bastard."

The king awoke to see the sparking light from the jeweled handle that pierced downward through his heart, cutting it asunder. He screamed in pain as he felt the blade slice through his chest. Jillian's betrayal was the last thing the dying monarch knew.

The happily avenged queen lay next to the king and gladly awaited her fate. She smiled, thinking of her beloved Markus. From within the shadows of the room, a dark cloud appeared. Jillian watched; the cloud rose above her, then descended slowly. She had been warned what to expect.

Knowing her time had come, she closed her eyes without a whimper. The black cloud was changing her body into a vapor that would vanish into history, never to be seen again.

Her wish for revenge upon the king was all she ever asked of the dagger, nothing more. The last time she met the wizard in her cell, she signed the agreement in her blood and said her goodbyes to the world where she no longer belonged.

Chapter 8

SETTING DOWN THE PARCHMENT, Melissa removed the gold-encrusted case. Its jewels sparkled in the fluorescent lights. Opening the small lid, she saw a familiar ancient weapon she hadn't seen in years. The Jillian Dagger was supposed to have been used in the ritual to kill her and bring the evil wizard Tobias back to life. *Why on earth would the professor send this disgusting thing to me?*

She saw something strange that she didn't expect. Examining the knife, she noticed human blood coated several jewels and dripped down the handle. She twirled the blade, taking the dagger from its case and allowing the gems to sparkle.

She thought of Tom Taylor—the cruel kid who became the murderer. Did this dagger mean Professor Etheridge figured she would need magical assistance again to defeat Tom? Did he have another sorcerer helping him this time or something worse?

She inadvertently touched the dagger's tip; it cut her. As she began bleeding, she thought, *If a demon is helping Tom, then what can mortals do if they had to battle the powerful fallen angel and hope to win? But they did win those years ago. Otherwise, my sister and I would have died!*

Taking the velvet cloth, she held it to her finger,

applying pressure to stop the bleeding. Something strange began to happen. She felt a connection to the instrument of death that seemed unexplainable as if it had tasted her blood. Together they became intertwined and connected through magical entitlements.

Holding the dagger in the light, she saw her blood run down its sharp edge. Suddenly, the blade began vibrating as if awakening from a long sleep. Melissa somehow knew it to mean one thing: Revenge, infused with forgotten magic, was now hers to command. She thought, *This powerful weapon was made to bring about my demise. Now, through a twisted act of fate, it is in my possession. Finally, I have something that will aid me in my fight to defend my family and find my father. Dad, where are you?*

Gripping the dagger, Melissa had a crystal clear realization. This artifact could not be wrapped up and stored in its box, left for another time or some other Bishop woman. This weapon, still as powerful as the day it was created, now belonged to her as an ancestor to the Bishop name, her family, the ones that always found themselves the product of sacrifice. No longer would a Bishop bow to the Taylor hoard. No longer would their blood be spilled to bring life to some damn sorcerer of the dark arts. No, this weapon would kill but no longer murder any innocent mortals. It would kill Tom Taylor. He was the one who would finally "own" this dagger. He was the one who would understand the sharpness of the blade when it was buried deep into his heart!

Before today, what little chance did any of them have to defeat dark magic? What could they do as mortals? If it weren't for Sterling and Stannis, Tom Taylor would have had their heads on pikes, never mind their children, the remaining offspring of the Bishop family. Something must be done; she could not just leave this blade lying around.

First and foremost, how could she explain to her husband the need to keep this dagger close, within reach, close enough to grab it at a moment's notice and thrust it into the heart of a monster? Now it seemed monsters were everywhere, popping out of the woodwork, ready to kill. Now she must be in the same mindset and be prepared to slaughter and thrust the knife into any evil creature imagined by Tom Taylor. *You bastard, what have you done with my father?* Weak and still mortal, the thoughts of her family careened down upon Melissa as if a rainy cloudburst.

As she suddenly began to weep, she thought of her mother, Barbara, and her inner strength and the remarkable way she faced death. Not a burden to anyone even when she could no longer walk, she still tried to perform such tasks as making the beds or preparing dinner for Mark. But soon she became bedridden and talked about her childhood life, never expecting to fight against evil.

If she wasn't a mortal human cursed with frailties that the entire world shared in these fragile bodies but had magical powers much like Stannis, the question was: How does one go about becoming a powerful wizard? She imagined the years of dedication to possess the inherited abilities to practice witchcraft. *Or is it as simple as a family trait locked into our blood through our genes?* No matter her desires, she was reduced to being an ordinary soccer mom and nothing else.

Now within her grasp, here and now, was an object of magic. Now she knew the complete story of Jillian and the king. All these characters were brought together—and defeated, she might add. Well, Tom Taylor will also defeat you like those before you.

What she did not yet know was what her part in the destruction of Tom would be. If only the authorities had done their part, he would have suffered the lethal injection, and the world would have been a better place because of it. But as it was, he was alive, and the only one responsible for taking her father, Mark, which was no doubt in her mind.

Now to the matter of the blade. No, it would never leave Melissa's side. No matter what. How to transport it was the question. She'd look silly going to the kids' school carrying a bejeweled knife. Although their lives could depend on it, she'd look foolish and probably get arrested. She had a thought: Her husband, Dan, was learning to become a blacksmith. He had his personal collection in his shop. She hurried out to the garage to look for some sort of sheath for the thing.

Dan's work filled the shed with strange burnt metal smells when she arrived at the forge. The remains of the last metal concoction he forged sat on the workbench, still in its rawest form, not resembling anything but junk metal. She knew it would be amazing once he did his grinding and sanding. As expected, other knives and sharp objects were proudly displayed on a board beside his workbench.

Seeing two possible pieces housed in their leather sheaths, Melissa took one off the display board. At first glance the knife looked close to the size of the dagger so, taking the blade out, she set it down on the table and inserted the Jillian Dagger inside. Still, her dagger was longer than the leather sheath so she took the next one down. There was something different about this sheath; it had a belt sewn in so it could be worn around your waist.

Removing the knife from the sheath, she slid the Jillian Dagger inside. A perfect match, a small leather hoop was already sown in, making the blade secure by wrapping the leather latch over the end of the handle. Next, grabbing the leather straps, Melissa wrapped the belt around her body and tightened the ends together. *Dan, you're a genius!* she thought. Twisting her body and jumping in the air, the weapon stayed, not moving.

Putting everything back except the sheath, she returned to the house and was about to begin her morning ritual. But before she did she went into their master bedroom. There in the mirror was her reflection in the bedroom dresser mirror. In her blue jeans and a baggy T-shirt, the shirt now covered the weapon so it was hidden.

She stood and looked at herself. She was studying her posture. Never in her life had she given so much attention to her stance. Could she learn to fight? Clean shirts and dinner would wait!

She was watching herself, studying her slow rhythmic movements. She swayed as if dancing with Dan in a romantic embrace. Unexpectedly, she stopped quickly, reached around, withdrew the dagger behind her back, and thrust it at an imaginary opponent! *Not too bad*, she thought, better than she could have imagined. Still, something about drawing the weapon seemed slow and sluggish.

I have no time for this. I need to practice to get it right, not by watching movies or imaginary villains but by real ones, out to kill, not make-believe.

Who could teach her? Who on earth had the time, with Tom popping up constantly trying to kill her and her family? There was no time for practice; she must hone her skills simultaneously.

A man close to fifty had attempted to teach her sons the fundamentals of self-defense; although they were more interested in playing video games, the man's words seemed intriguing. She remembered her sons' karate instructor, John. She hadn't had time to participate in the lessons but was very interested in what he had to say.

Was this it? Was she to be the one to keep her family safe, all by herself? Yes, she always had help from psychic detective Sterling. And after all this time his actual name was finally revealed: Sebastian Martin! Who would have guessed? Sebastian, no wonder he changed his name. No matter, back to the thought of training. She walked over, grabbed her phone book, and thumbed through the pages until she found John Goertz, the martial arts instructor, and his phone number. Without hesitation, she dialed the number and waited. A short time later she heard a familiar man's voice.

"This is John. How may I help you?"

Thinking to herself the words she most wanted to hear, Melissa responded, "Mr. Goertz, I'm not sure if you remember me, but my name is Melissa Carpenter. You taught my two sons a couple of years ago."

"Yes, of course, Mark and David. Tell me, how are the boys doing?"

"They're fine. But truthfully, it's not my sons I'm calling about. It's me."

"Yes, go on."

"Listen, John, I'm not sure how to say this, but a need has arisen, and I need your help. What I mean to say is I need a crash course in self-defense training, and I don't have much time." She paused. "I'm worried about my family, my sons. I believe they are in grave danger!"

"What type of danger, Mrs. Carpenter? What do you mean?"

"I don't like to bring up the past, but did you ever hear about what happened to my sister and me?"

"I'm afraid I don't know what you mean."

"As young girls, my sister and I were kidnapped by a psycho named Martin Taylor It was in all the newspapers."

"Yes, I'd be lying if I said I didn't hear about this. Yes, go on."

"I fear this could happen again. You see, the son of the Taylor family was released from prison not that long ago. Oh my god, Mr. Goertz, could you help me? Will you help me?"

"Oh, I see."

"Truly, I hope you do because there is no time for testing for belts and meeting other students for practice. I need to learn what is most important about how to protect myself and my family in case a kidnapper or villain confronts me!"

"Please tell me, Mrs. Carpenter, the training you speak is rarely taught to novices and requires a rigid discipline, allowing for no excuses. If you fail to miss just one class, I cannot help you further and will terminate our agreement. You will be on your own."

"Mr. Goertz, you have my word. How soon can we begin?"

"No longer will you refer to me as sir. From this time forward, you will refer to me as Sensei. Your training has already begun. I hope you know what you're doing, Mrs. Carpenter. I will not show you pity."

"Sensei, I bow before you as a new student, putty in your hands to do with me as you wish. I shall not whimper or cry. It's too late for that. Now I fight!"

"Yes, be prepared to fight. I promise you it won't be easy. You have my word!"

"Nothing about my life has been easy ever since that day when men dressed in black clothing decided to steal away my innocence. I will not allow this to happen again. No, not to my sons. I will see you in the morning, Sensei. Thank you."

Chapter 9

HEATHER DROPPED HER SON off at the babysitter's before arriving at her job. She worked at the coffee house on a corner of a busy boulevard downtown. Inside a line of patrons was already waiting to place their orders. She walked back behind the counter. Avery and Jenny were busily taking orders while Anita made an espresso drink for a customer.

The hectic schedule was an everyday occurrence. Heather had worked at this tiny coffee bar for the past three years before her divorce from her husband, Nicholas Drexel, over his constant infidelities. She held onto her job as the only means of income for both her and eleven-month-old Noah. Raising a child on her own proved difficult, but so did keeping awake at night wondering if her husband would come home smelling like booze and cheap perfume. She was better off by herself.

Within the next few hours, the line of customers began to thin out. The small crowd inched forward. Next in line was an older woman carrying a large black leather purse. Her hair was bleached a bright red. She stood barely five feet tall. When she approached the counter, Jenny smiled while asking for her order. The woman smiled back.

"Heather Taylor, please."

Clearing tables behind her, Heather replied, "I'm Heather Taylor. Can I help you? Wait a minute, aren't you Grandmother Della? You're still alive! I thought I had lost you! Oh, my heavens, where have you been?" Heather screamed out with excitement.

Turning to address the young hostess, Della said, "Heather, my dear, I'm so glad to find you at last."

The woman walked up to Heather, grabbed her hand, then placed a jeweled diamond ring around her finger.

Staring at the expensive item that resembled a rose, Heather saw all manner of jewels set in pure gold. The diamond must have been over ten carats, surrounded by sapphires and rubies reflecting radiantly. It must be worth a king's ransom. Heather stood speechless, admiring the costly prize.

"This belonged to your great-great-grandmother, Eve."

Still in shock, Heather was flooded with many questions. But looking at the woman's fragility, she hurriedly grabbed a chair and suggested that Della take a seat.

"Can I get you anything? Perhaps a sweet roll or something?" Heather asked while looking at her grandmother both lovingly and nervously. The ring hung heavily on her hand, making her feel even more out of place.

"Yes, that would be nice, honey. But please don't go to any trouble for me."

"What! Are you kidding me? Trouble, no way. At last I have found you. All this time I thought you had passed away. Oh my God, can you believe it?" Heather announced to the customers who had become careless spectators to this unusual family reunion.

Her co-workers surrounded her, giving hugs and examining the trinket on her finger like an engagement ring.

Within minutes Heather returned with the best sweet roll they had in stock. Sitting next to her grandmother, she watched her take a small bite.

"That's good. Thank you."

Heather stared at her, and the tears suddenly ran down her cheeks. No, not tears of sadness she was accustomed to, but tears of joy to finally be connected with a living relative.

Della reached for her hand, gently squeezing it and assuring her she was no longer alone, especially since losing all her family except her murderous brother, Tom.

"I'm sure you have all kinds of questions. I can assure you they all will be answered. First, let me say what a beautiful woman you have grown up to become. Your grandfather would be so proud," Della said while handing Heather a tissue.

"Grandfather Taylor, I barely knew him. I can hardly remember his funeral. I was so young when he passed away."

"I'm so glad I found you, Heather. The truth be told, I've been searching for you ever since I discovered your family was lost in that fire. But I was hampered by an illness that sent me to the hospital and eventually placed me in a coma. I could only figure out that it wasn't my time to die. I even told those damn doctors as much when I awoke. Sadly, I discovered a decade had passed, and your whereabouts were unknown."

"I was married once. I changed my name," Heather explained.

"That's why I contacted a private eye."

"You actually used a private investigator to find me?" Heather replied.

"Before that fire happened I tried talking to your father's wife, Eileen, to ask how you and your siblings were doing. That woman wanted nothing to do with the Taylor family or me. Once I awoke from my coma, I became desperate to find your whereabouts. You must believe me."

"I have no doubts, grandmother. All I can say is that when it comes to Eileen, none of us kids liked the woman. We could never figure out what our father saw in her. She was harsh to all us kids, especially me. I wouldn't tolerate any of her abuse."

"Abuse, you say? That's troubling to hear. Why on earth would Martin allow such treatment of his children? I'll never know."

"Oh, let me tell you. There was one in the family that Eileen adored. For whatever reason she considered Tommy the son she never had. I remember one incident while Dad was gone when Eileen gave Tommy some alcohol. She enjoyed seeing him drunk. As a result, he spent the night worshipping the ivory commode."

"She should have been arrested," Della responded while taking another bite of her sweet roll.

"My older sister Anita wasn't amused; she told her as much. Regardless, Eileen still saw the whole affair as humorous, telling my sister that Tommy had to experience a taste of the good life. Can you imagine the nerve of that woman?"

"The world is better for her passing. I hate to say this about someone, but I cannot help it. Yes, she was hateful. But the truth is you cannot argue about who your son takes as a wife; you can only offer your advice. Martin wanted none of mine, I'm afraid."

"When he met her, he fell deeply in love, or was it lust?" Heather responded.

"Well, I'm not sure, honey. Alright, enough of the past. Let's talk about the future. About a week ago I received a correspondence from Hancock. He told me where to find you. Time is short; I have much to say about our family. There is no time to waste."

"Please listen, I cannot return to recapture my youth; I'm close to thirty years old. The past doesn't amount to a hill of beans; you're here now—that's all that matters."

"I'm glad to hear you say that. I have a question to ask you. Are you free to have dinner with me this evening?"

"As a matter of fact, Noah and I are free this evening, other than doing laundry, making baby formula, that sort of thing," Heather announced with laughter.

"You have a son? Hancock never put that in the report. Oh, how thrilling. I can't wait to meet our little man. Please write down your address for me. I'll have my car pick you up around six."

"Yes, of course," Heather remarked, removing a piece of paper from her apron, taking a pen from her top pocket, and jotting down her address. She handed it to Della and said, "I'm so glad you finally found me. You have no idea what this means to me,"

"I'm glad you accepted my gift. I wasn't sure what I would have done if you had refused it. It's your legacy, you know." Della said.

"All I know was the family curse associated with the Taylor name. I remember the last time we spoke; I was in eighth grade. Never in my wildest dreams would I have guessed that something as luxurious as this diamond ring could ever be mine. Even today I wasn't sure why you left me that old book on the Taylor family, but it did become useful when I needed it to explain events involving the curse to a grieving mother," Heather responded.

Reaching to hold Heather's hand, Della modestly said, "Dearie, you haven't seen anything yet."

Then she picked up her heavy purse and left the coffee house in a waiting car.

EVERYONE AT THE COFFEE BAR was so pleased that she had connected with her family that she thought had vanished completely. Turning back to face her co-workers, everyone stood with gaping mouths, unsure how to respond to their friend's good fortune. Heather excused herself for the rest of the day once Della left. It wouldn't be proper etiquette to look like a hillbilly; she had to shop for a new dress.

Before she left the coffee bar, she cautiously removed the expensive ring and placed it inside her purse. She didn't want to walk around town with the item exposed or take the chance that it could get stolen. However, when she stepped outside onto the sidewalk to her car, she felt like someone was watching her.

She unlocked the door when she reached her car and quickly got inside. Starting her engine, she gave it a few minutes to warm up. Heather had parked off the main boulevard next to an office building. Its large glass windows mirrored her reflection. Looking across the sidewalk, she saw her likeness in her car. Behind her in the window's reflection, a pair of red eyes stared at her. She gasped.

Opening her car, she quickly shot out of the driver's seat, stood in the street, and gawked back at the back seat where she had seen the ghostly image. An oncoming car honked its horn, scaring her further. Springing to the curb, she waved her apologies to the driver. Now she stood outside her car, refusing to get inside. Holding her purse tightly, she wasn't sure what to do. However, one fact remained: She knew she wasn't getting back into that car.

After several minutes she thought to call her friend Peggie. When Peggie answered the phone, Heather told her that her car was giving her trouble and asked her for a ride home.

"Sure, I'm on my way," Peggy announced.

While waiting Heather stood beside her car, gathering the courage to return to the driver's seat and shut off the engine. Pedestrians walking by gave her strange looks seeing the terrified expression on her face.

When she saw Peggie turn the corner, she no longer hesitated—jumping into the driver's seat of her car, expecting the bogeyman to leap upon her at any moment. She shut off the engine and hurried out again. As Peggie pulled into space a couple of cars down from her, Heather took her car keys, locked the car, and gladly walked away.

On the way to Heather's house, they approached the mall entrance. Heather asked if it wasn't too inconvenient that they make a quick stop at the mall. She explained that she was going there when something happened to her car.

Peggie asked, "Is it the fuel pump again, like last time?"

Heather replied, "No, something much different. Look, I'm not comfortable getting back inside that car, that's all."

Thinking it strange, Peggie pulled into a parking

place near the mall entrance. Shutting off the engine, she turned to face her friend. "What does that mean you're not comfortable getting into your car? Hello, it's your car!" she remarked, demanding an answer.

"Alright, listen, you're going to think I'm nutty. I just know it."

"No, not me. Tell me, how long have we known one another? Remember I was there in high school when you lost your entire family. Everyone thought you were weird; they refused to be your friend. Honestly, you can tell me anything!"

"Alright, but you have to know that today has been strange. First, I visited my long-lost Grandmother Della, who wants me to come for dinner this evening. She gave me this! Looking deep into the hidden compartment inside her purse, Heather withdrew the diamond ring. The jewels exposed to sunlight were dazzling. Peggie`s mouth completely dropped open; no words came out.

Heather continued telling her story of the strange set of eyes in the back seat of her car. Again, Peggie was speechless.

"Now I have to find a dress for this evening. Can you please help me?" Heather said.

"Oh, sure, I think. Oh my heavens, you can't enter the mall with that diamond ring. People will shoot you and take it from your cold dead body. But please listen to me."

"What can I do?"

"Wait a minute; I have an idea. What if we take it to my bank and store it temporarily inside a safety deposit box? For a short time, mind you. When we're done we'll return to the bank to retrieve the ring."

"Sure, that sounds like a plan. That's a way better idea than what I came up with doing. All I would do was store it in your car's trunk."

"No, no, that will never do. Geez, the value of that thing. Just imagine for a minute if someone stole my car; they would retire for life."

Starting her car again, they left the mall's parking lot and drove to Peggie's bank a mile down the road. When they arrived Peggie got out, watching for any strange-looking characters. Heather, too, looked around for anyone following them, then gripped her purse and hurried inside.

After stashing the ring in Peggie's safety deposit box, they returned to the mall. Melissa tried on several dresses and finally went with one of Peggie's favorites. They returned to the bank where the teller helping them was Peggie's cousin, Beth. She had thought it a joke when they said they'd be back within the hour, and now she was very curious about what they had put in the safety deposit box. But after heading back to the safe one more time, the ring was back in Heather's possession, Peggie drove her to the babysitter's to pick up Noah, then home.

Peggie explained that she had to get home before her husband got off work, then hugged her friend and sped away. While saying their goodbyes, Peggie promised to have her phone on if she was needed again.

Time slipped through Heather's fingers as if it were sand as she fed, dressed, and packed Noah's diaper bag. There was a knock on her front door as she put on her final makeup touches. She glanced through the peephole and saw a man dressed all in black, wearing a suit and black chauffeur's hat.

Leaving her apartment, she and Noah sat comfortably in the black leather rear seat. Noah quickly fell asleep in the car seat. Heather felt herself relax as if she had arrived where she belonged. After a while the car followed a long, winding road littered with mansions of various sizes. The limo pulled up to a high iron gate and stopped. She heard the driver conversing with someone through a microphone mounted on a brick podium with a statue on top of a man riding a horse. The gate swung open, and the chauffeur drove the car inside.

Heather was amazed at the size of the property as the car pulled up to the entrance. She saw two large marble lions on display under lights illuminating the curved driveway. The lone mother unbuckled her son as the chauffeur opened the car door. Existing in the limousine, she stood holding Noah and gazed at her surroundings. The mansion was at least four stories high. It had stained glass windows. Along the roof, stone gargoyles eyed any would-be visitors.

Della stood wearing a smile at the top of a set of stairs leading to the large front doors. "I'm so glad to see you, my dear. You brought a special guest to see his great-grandmother."

Reaching the top of the stairs, Heather hugged Della warmly. She lifted her son and said, "Please let me introduce my handsome little man Noah. He turns a year old next week."

The child, waking up from sleep, looked up at Della and smiled.

Della was thrilled; it had been years since she had had a baby to dote on.

Heather, smelling something unpleasant, excused herself and said, "I'm sorry, but do you have a bathroom? I'm quite sure a diaper needs changing."

"Yes, of course. Come with me."

Afterward, they retired to the library. The evening was divine, and the dinner was delicious. A glass of sherry was poured, and family memories of happier times were discussed. Hearing stories of her mother brought mixed emotions to Heather. When she listened to the accounts of her mother's death, Heather was reminded of those dark days she tried to forget.

Time passed quickly—the evening was getting late. Heather was shown a guest bedroom and asked to stay the night. Della said she wanted to capture every moment of happiness she could, having so little time left her. Besides, Della wanted to get to know little Noah better. Without argument, Heather agreed but said that in the morning she would have to retrieve her abandoned vehicle from the streets before it got towed.

After ringing a bell, a man appeared. After receiving directions to Heather's car's location, he took the keys and disappeared. Della suggested that Heather allow her to handle it.

"I have servants to handle that situation," Della explained.

Heather sat on the expensive carpet with her grandmother, who enjoyed playing with Noah.

After hearing the story about the set of red eyes in her back seat, Della responded. "Yes, your brother Tom is acting like a little shit, isn't he? I warned Martin about that boy; he was born under a bad sign."

"Grandmother, why would you blame Tom for this? I haven't spoken to him in years, especially since my divorce."

"Surely you have felt his presence lurking around, haven't you? No, there's more to that curse than meets the eye."

"What do you mean?"

"Your brother has become a mighty sorcerer. He must be stopped from destroying those poor Bishops."

"Wait a minute, grandmother, I thought all that business was over. I expected to go about my life without worrying about that damn curse."

"Heather, I have to ask you, haven't you been following the newspaper articles about your brother?"

"Actually, no. I refused to hear anything about the murderous Tom Taylor! Once I changed my name, I hoped to dissolve my connection with the Taylor family. This name change is best for my son because I don't want his life ruined by knowing his uncle is a psychopath."

"It's time, I suppose. You have to know the real reason I have sought you out."

"What do you mean, grandmother?"

"Yes, I worried about what happened to you after the fire. I never expected that we would be together again like now, but there is also something that I must give to you. I would feel relieved once this object is in your possession."

"Just being here with you is treasure enough. I don't need expensive stuff. Just your love."

"That is yours to have. However, that is not what I'm saying. I wish it were that simple but it's not."

"Now I'm confused. What do you mean?"

"Tom, your brother, is not the only one with experience with the supernatural. The ability to harness the powers of magic is a gift known to a select few. Someone powerful enough to destroy an entire monarchy is extremely rare. I'm talking about the black plague and other historical events."

"I read the accounts of the curse between our families in the book you gave me. Grayson Taylor wrote that. He described events that provided an entire legacy, but no one ever said anything about entire civilizations being destroyed."

Suddenly, a dark cloud appeared in the room. Out of it, a man's hand gripped Heather around her neck and began to choke her. Della, seeing the apparition, sprang into action. Grabbing hold of Noah, she screamed out to her maid. A woman in her sixties appeared in the room. Della pushed Noah at her.

"Take him to a safe place."

Once the maid was gone, Della stood next to a photograph of Tom that she had placed in the room and said a few words. Then Tom stepped into the room from the dark swirling cloud. His grip on Heather's neck never faltered. He lifted Heather off the floor; she couldn't breathe and was beginning to turn blue.

"Dear sister, Heather, we finally meet again, not behind bars as you left me. No, now I'm free and alive, with powers unimaginable. Even though you are my sister, the lone survivor of the once proud Taylor clan, I choose not to forgive you for your betrayal. I'm here to destroy both you and your brat."

"Tom, please, I beg you," Heather's muffled voice squeaked out.

"I'm sorry, I'm not in the business of forgiving. Not you or any surviving Bishops. I have already destroyed Barbara Bishop, the mommy to those little bitches. Mark, their father, is dead now, too. His corpse I discarded at the Whisper Pines resort. He'll be found soon enough, but the prime glory will be to destroy Melissa's twin boys. Their blood will be used to save my offspring born with the Taylor family defect."

In this war against evil magic, one instrument lay forgotten. Tom was too busy gloating over his powers and didn't think about Della. But the woman was watching everything. She knew what to do.

Only a few feet away from where a moment ago she was enjoying the company of her granddaughter was a secret compartment. With no time to waste, she quickly glanced back at Heather, whose eyes were closed. Tom, the fool, continued blabbing on about how he would inherit the world.

Della desperately began touching individual switches in the distinctive pattern on the shelf, and a small drawer popped open. Grabbing the object inside, Della took it and hurried to where Tom was standing. The Mother's Regret Crystal instantly illuminated and came to life. It was the crystal that Sterling had given to Barbara to protect her children from the dark sorcerer Tobias. How Della had come to own it was a story for another time. For now, she needed to wield it against her grandson. The radiant brilliance blasted the room with sparkling light. Tom dropped Heather to the floor; repulsed by the brightness, his powers vanquished.

Della held the crystal, approached, and ordered Tom to leave her home. He couldn't stand the light.

Squinting his eyes, he placed his arm in front of his face. "Curse you, you old bitch. How did you find that damn crystal? Remove it or I will destroy you."

"Tom, you cursed little imp. I order you to leave. Do it now."

Della brought the crystal closer to the man; she wanted to touch him. But regrettably, a portal erupted across the room, and Tom withdrew inside the dark cloud and vanished before her sight.

Racing to Heather's side, Della knelt. Grabbing hold of her granddaughter, she called out her name, hoping to see her eyes open. Heather gasped for breath and began to cough. Seeing the red bruises around Heather's neck, Della knew her granddaughter would have died if she could not chase her grandson away. Procuring the Mother Regret Crystal many years ago was a wise decision.

Tom, her grandson, had become too powerful. Seeing how he could enter any dwelling without resistance was frightening. He had to be stopped. But how?

Suddenly, Heather sat up and cried out for Noah.

"He's safe, honey. Don't worry. I have him where no one can find him. I'm worried for you. How are you?"

"Tom, that bastard, tried to kill me. He would have, too, if not for that strange object you brought to stop him. What was that thing exactly?"

Still holding the crystal in her hand, Della displayed it before Heather. "I believe you have seen this before."

"I haven't, but I think I know what it is from the stories in the Taylor family chronicles."

"Please listen to me. I've lived a long time, Heather. Seeing both you and Noah has made my life complete. If Tom had killed you tonight, he would have taken away all the happiness I have in this life. That is why I want you to have this."

She placed the cord that held the crystal around Heather's neck and kissed her forehead, whispering something faint and hard to understand. Heather felt exhilarated, although she couldn't explain why.

Standing, Della said, "Let's go get our little boy and put all this behind us."

Following Della, they walked down a long hallway that ended at some stairs that descended underneath the house. Heather's throat began to spasm, and she coughed. After a few minutes she gently touched her throat. It felt raw. It had started to swell and was very sore. Tom's chokehold would surely leave a bruise around her neck.

The evil that had appeared was again overpowered and beaten. Heather's throat began to cool as she followed her grandmother to a secret chamber within the mansion's walls. The sharp pain that was there each time she swallowed disappeared as if by magic, and she felt healed completely. It seemed the crystal she wore around her neck had unique powers.

Now she noticed a slow, rhythmic hum vibrating from the crystal, which she felt throughout her body. Forever connected with the magical object, she knew she could never take it off. No, not as long as Tom was alive. The fact that her brother was indeed a monster the world would grow to fear was a horrible reality.

Previously, she could never accept what everyone said about him; she'd been sure she could help him see the light. But now the fact that she could have easily lost her only son to this monster was a devastating realization. She knew that Tom Taylor, her brother, must die.

Chapter 10

Ever since he was punched in the jaw by Tom Taylor, Sterling had noticed that his psychic abilities were waning, finding it difficult to see into the spiritual realm. He felt useless; his psychic skills were needed, yet he could no longer close his eyes and picture what was on the other side of the curtain.

That's why he'd sought out Stannis, only to find the man was missing, at best, or perhaps even dead. Melissa and Rachel needed him, and he had been reduced to a mere human.

There had been no news of Mark, their father. Sterling was sure he was dead; his corpse would be discovered when Tom wanted them to find it.

Finding himself alone, he tried to resist searching out the woman whose name he had heard in his vision. It was an itch that he couldn't stop scratching. He was, after all, a detective of sorts, even though he'd never worn a badge. He didn't need one to know how to sniff out a clue. He had been doing it all his life or most of his life. Sterling, the psychic detective—right?

The itch continued. Sterling stared at the computer. Finally, he logged in and began typing. Oh, that name. Ms. Cornwall. His only other clue? His favorite island, St. Thomas. He stared at the blank screen. Now what? Too many questions. Where to begin? She could live anywhere in the world. Damn it—these questions. His index finger continued to tap on the keyboard. Children, the children, yes, about the children. What about the children? Hitting the question mark key repeatedly, Sterling repeated the word children. Okay, the children, were they his and hers? Offspring from a dead husband? Or divorce? *Shit, I need a drink*!

After standing and walking away from the damn computer, Sterling entered his kitchen and grabbed a crystal glass from the cupboard. Stopping at the refrigerator, he dropped in a couple of ice cubes. Walking into his study, he stopped at his bar and grabbed a bottle of his favorite scotch. Pouring the glass full, he stood there briefly and took a drink. Another thought popped into his head: *What if the children are someone else's, and they hate me? Even worse, what if they think I'm stupid and not cool or hip?* Sighing, he took another sip. Returning to his bottle, he refilled his glass and whispered, "A father? Me, Sterling, a father? No. Yes, why not?"

Feeling tipsy, he grabbed the bottle, returned to his office, and sat at the computer again. He placed his glass on a coaster. He began his search.

Damn, another thought, *spoiler alert!* Was it wise to find Ms. Cornwall and try to meet her in her world? What if she was still happily married? He could picture it all. Dummy appears on her doorstep, saying, "Hello there, baby cakes, what's up?" She screams. He's thrown in jail for being what? A stalker? Sterling the Stalker! Oh shit, that's just great!

By this time he had consumed enough alcohol to feel a little brave—perhaps too courageous? Casting his worries aside, he opened a search engine and typed "Ms. Cornwall." The search was too broad; he knew that.

Thousands of images appeared on the screen, primarily from various social media. Another reality struck him as he examined the pages; he wasn't sure what she looked like. The woman in his vision had worn a black and gold one-piece bathing suit. Her hair had been concealed under a sizeable straw hat; he wasn't sure about the color. Her legs, yes. Those long, shapely legs. Ok, ok, he drew a deep breath. Somewhat distracted, he thought of her face, a small nose, bright smile. Oh, her smile made him melt on the spot. And her voice, was there an accent? *Oh, Sterling, my boy, you got it bad!*

Just then Mr. Bigglesworth brushed against him, demanding attention. He began to pet him softly on his head while staring at the computer. Too much information was splattered across the screen, making him more confused. Taking his mouse, he thumbed through the results, cursing Tom Taylor for his debilitating spell. He'd easily spot her among the crowd if he had clairvoyant abilities. Bam! If his abilities had still been working, he'd know who she was. He would make a simple call to his friend Jack, and within a day he'd have the complete breakdown of her criminal history. Shit, criminal. Why would he think she was a criminal? No, she couldn't be. *Hey, what the hell? Who cares if Ms. Cornwall has a record, right?*

Sterling was not a fan of social media where people did nothing but showed off to their family and friends. Putting so much personal information on display went against his grain. Still, finding old friends or keeping up with what's happening in the family couldn't be discounted. Sterling had no family; he had nothing to announce to the world. He was an introvert. What if she's a social butterfly and every time they went out to dinner she was busily snapping pictures to broadcast what she ate for dinner on the web? His life suddenly splattered all over the web for everyone to see. This relationship thing could have its downsides.

But love, yes, unconditional love meant encompassing every part of her, including being a "Chatty Cathy" on the web! If their love were complete, she would understand him like no other, and she would know his quirky side, his profound telepathic travels from this world into the next. She would appreciate Sterling. The children. Again, he went back to the children. What type of parent would he be? Damn, the questions! Damn his inquisitive mind!

Trust and hope the children would learn about their father, whether step or otherwise. Love had been a forgotten word in Sterling's life, a meaningless word until that vision. Could it be that he'd been daydreaming of a happier life all this time, and it was all a farce?

The "what if" game continued to flash in his thoughts. What if there was no Ms. Cornwall? What if Tom Taylor made it all up? What if the vision of happy days ahead was a farce Tom Taylor had called up to distract him? Sterling sighed. He soberly clicked off the computer, cursing the weakness that had made him hope there was love in his future. Damn his mortal desires to feel love and want love, like everyone else on this miserable planet.

Silent and all alone, he stood and walked to his bedroom. Stripping naked, he crawled beneath the silk sheets. Laying his head upon the soft pillow, he thought of Ms. Cornwall, her happy smile, her silky words announcing her name as Mrs. Sterling. And her motherly attention to the children. It had been nothing more than a trick, a hook, to catch the man, the psychic who goes by the name of Sterling.

Chapter 11

A CALL CAME INTO THE STATION sometime in the morning hours. The caretaker at the Whisper Pines resort in the Catskills Mountains reported that he had discovered a body. Two seasoned detectives, Schneider and Jones, responded to the call. When they arrived at the resort's entrance, a policeman was parked near the road, blocking anyone from disturbing the gruesome remains at the crime scene.

When the detectives drove down the old, crumbled road toward where the body was located, Jones remarked, "Hey, this place looks familiar. I worked a case here years ago when I was a rookie. It involved the kidnapping of a teenage girl. The good news is that the mother found the kid alive; they even captured the guy in the process."

"I heard about that case when I transferred into homicide. Didn't the family get help from the well-known psychic Sterling?"

"Yeah, the mom claimed that this kid named Tommy Taylor was the mastermind behind the kidnapping, but it didn't seem plausible. I know Taylor killed his siblings—set the house on fire. But how could he do that and be at the resort to kidnap the girl? To me, it seemed that the victims we interviewed were hiding something. I don't know; the whole thing seemed like a fantasy, especially when we separated the girls from their mom. They babbled on about magical wizards, a dragon, and spiders. I figured it was PTSD or something. But damn, hearing all that crap kept me awake for weeks. It scared the shit out of me, I admit."

"Jones, listen to me: Whoever was behind the kidnapping no doubt spiked the Kool-Aid they were drinking with some hallucinogenic drug."

"I pray you're right. That's all I'm saying."

Soon they arrived at the ruins of the Whisper Pines resort, parking near where a sergeant named Peters stood. He directed them to where the body was lying next to the wall.

They approached the body lying on a crumbled tiled floor. The spectacle was gruesome, but in police work such a sight wasn't the worst any of the detectives had seen.

The head of a man was seated upon a rock. The man's arms had been cut off his torso and were now arranged in opposite directions, one lying west and the other east. The rest of the body was lying directly south. Stepping closer, Jones stooped down and examined the remains. He looked at the man's head. His eyes were burned out of his skull. A black oozing liquid dripped outward from the head, down the cheeks. A pentagram was burned into the forehead.

Jones took notes to be compiled later in the report when the Crime Scene Investigation (CSI) unit arrived. After getting out of the van, one man began taking pictures, and another set up small plastic numbered markers near any possible evidence.

There were two sets of tiny footprints and one large. A stretch limo was parked nearby. It had been used to bring the victim to the scene. *What a bizarre choice,*

Jones thought. *And why leave it?* Photos were collected of the pathway in relation to the body's remains, the surrounding buildings, and the small kitchen area where they found drug paraphernalia and a discarded bottle of whiskey.

After examining the torso, the time of death had been determined to be about a week before. The remains were swabbed for any trace amounts of chemicals. There were deep incisions in the body, numbering close to thirty. All this was documented in CSI's report.

When the CSI team concluded their investigation, the detectives were given the green light to examine the remains further.

Detective Jones returned to the corpse's head, sitting upon a rock. He examined the stone and noted the unusual designs, tiny stars, and different pentagrams that decorated the rock. The remains of the candles were set in a circular pattern that looked like an eight-pointed star.

"There must have been a ritual performed here, and a rather gruesome one at that," Jones said, turning to his partner.

When one of the crime lab investigators appeared, Schneider began questioning him about what he'd discovered.

"After a quick examination of the body, I noticed that, apart from being mutilated, the victim was alive when tortured, eventually dying from blood loss. His head was removed after his death due to evidence suggesting the lack of blood around the two sources, the internal carotid and vertebral arteries. The darkish liquid dripping from the eye sockets looks and smells like rotting putrid flesh," said Reese, the CSI investigator.

"What can you tell us about the hands? I noticed

they were missing, along with the man's eyes," Jones asked.

"Yes, the man's eyes were burned out of their sockets. If you prefer, the octave or cranial nerve seems to be removed entirely, which tells us a fire or something hot was used to remove the eyes. The heat source is pure speculation, but I believe it was a tool of some sort from the gouge marks left behind in the skull. Evidence also suggests that the victim's nerves should have been destroyed. From a quick glimpse and from what I can tell, the entire eye and octave nerves were removed together."

"Hum, why would someone want a guy's eyeballs?" Jones asked.

"Yes, who knows? But when it comes to the hands, they were removed with a sharp object. A clean cut, no mystery there," Reese explained.

"Well, identifying the guy without fingerprints will be a pain. We'll have to use dental records or look through the many missing person bulletins back at the station," Schneider announced.

Two men from the coroner's office arrived, pushing a gurney. They wore blue jeans and t-shirts with "coroner" printed in bold letters on their backs. They briefly studied the scattered remains. After returning to their van, they changed into plastic coveralls, stretched latex gloves over their hands, and adjusted masks over their faces. After pushing a gurney across the cracked tile ground, they again approached the scene, carrying black plastic bags. They heaved the torso inside a large, black body bag and deposited it atop the gurney. Walking over to the head, one of the men held open the plastic sack while the other bent to lift the chair free from the rock. It refused to budge. Looking at his partner, the man gave an odd grin, thinking about what could hold the thing in place.

The detectives watched with curiosity. Something wasn't right. A cold shiver ran down Jones' spine. Why was the coroner's man having such difficulty removing the head?

The man leaned closer to give a final heave. Using all his might, he pulled hard, placing his foot against the rock. Suddenly, the stone and head lifted from the ground, still bound together by some mysterious force.

There was a popping sound as the head slowly broke apart from the hard surface. A black oozing liquid gushed out, splashing the man's shoes, and a dark swarm of wasps flew out from under the skull, biting the man repeatedly as he held the head aloft. Boils appeared on the man's cheeks and forehead. He collapsed to the ground, dropping the head; it rolled slightly, lying sideways on the broken tiles.

As the swarming insects stung, the officer, Schneider, and Jones raced into what looked like a small office connected to the kitchen adjacent to the crime scene, locking themselves behind a small security door.

Safe inside, they gawked out the window. A swirling black cloud already covered the coroner's assistant. Seconds later he collapsed to the ground like his co-worker.

The police sergeant, Peters, observing the two men collapse, unholstered his gun and shot at the horde. A hole in the middle of the swarm was blown apart, but just as quickly the flying bugs rejoined formation and flew at the man unabated.

Peters yelled, "What! I have never met a demon," just as the swarm surrounded him, then he fell to the ground, unconscious.

Reese and his partner from the crime lab, seeing the effect of the biting insects, had run back to their van and sped off. Schneider and Jones stayed where they were. Afraid to move, they stood trembling in their place of safety. Hardened detectives they might have been, but this was different; no one knew how to respond to the evil manifestation.

"What are we going to do?" Jones asked.

"Look!" Schneider pointed.

The disembodied head had begun twitching and moving.

"What the hell is that?"

"Oh shit, what now?" Jones groaned.

As they watched, the head seemed to grow legs. Eight black thin, slender appendages grew out of it. Struggling to stand erect, it moved side to side until it realized the total weight of its birthing container. After a short time the legs positioned themselves directly under the head and sustained the heavy burden. The skull wobbled only slightly, then came to a stop. They stared, frozen in fear, as the head began to scamper toward the men lying on the ground. The spidery creature approached the police sergeant. Its thin, prickly legs scurried about excitedly. Reaching the man's legs, it climbed aboard and followed them up to his body, past his chest, arriving at Peters' face. A blank expression on the man's face suggested that he was someplace else. Schneider hoped he wasn't aware of what was happening to him.

The creature used two long, spidery legs to push the skull off its body. As it did so, its crown began to appear. It was entirely black. Its dome was round, with dozens of red openings that resembled eye sockets. Finally, free of the skull, the lifeless object rolled down the officer's body onto the ceramic tiles, stopping abruptly in an upright position.

It crawled upon Peters' face. A single long red spike appeared at the bottom of the spider's abdomen; it looked to be about four inches in size. Suddenly, the barb began punching a hole in the man's forehead. Blood splattered the man's face, dripping onto the floor. The spider moved in a circular pattern as it dug deeper into the man's head until, at last, pieces of brain matter began to shoot out of the hole. Its punishment was relentless. In no time at all it had drilled a hole entirely through.

The man's body twitched incessantly. His fingers on his hands jerked about until, at last, the creature had finished. It stopped and glanced back. Seeing no visible threat, it moved its round abdomen above the hole and began depositing something like green eggs.

Next, it traveled over to the other two men. This time something strange and different happened. Instead of punching a hole into the men's forehead, it crawled upward onto their bodies and began to spin greenish webs. When it had finished it crawled a few feet away and disappeared down a sewer drain.

The men whose bodies were coated with the spidery web began to send off a toxic white cloud. Apparently, it was a sort of acid—the web's material was acidic—and as Jones and Schneider watched it began to erode their organic tissue.

"What the hell was that?" Jones cried aloud.

"You're asking me," Schneider replied.

"I'm not sure, but the spider and the black wasps have disappeared."

"That's all well and good, but I'm not going outside."

"I'm not either. Look what happened to the guy holding the head."

Jones grabbed his cell phone. "I guess I better call the captain, but what in the hell should I say to him? This whole thing sounds crazy!"

"No kidding, but we should call the Centers for Disease Control and Prevention (CDC). There might be an outbreak of some rare disease that will come from the three men's bodies," Schneider suggested.

"Yes, alright, first I'll call the captain, then the CDC. It looks like it's going to be a long night."

Taking out a cigarette, he tried to light the end, but his hand shook so badly; he struggled to get the end lit. Finally successful, he took his first drag.

"Damn it, how in the hell will we explain what we just saw to anyone else? Who in their right mind would believe us?" Jones said as he turned to Schneider.

"Wait, hold on a minute, brother! The guys from the crime lab will back our stories."

"Reese! That's right; he saw it all. That should convince Captain Edwards that it's not a figment of our imaginations."

"I hope so. Damn it, this whole thing is turning into a real shitstorm," Schneider replied.

Jones couldn't get the picture of the men dying out of his head, and how they had been helpless to intervene. He took another drag and proclaimed, "I wish I had stayed home."

"Forget it, pal. You're with me on this one."

"Alright, I'll make the call."

Taking his cell phone, he dialed the number to the station. "This is Detective Jones, is the captain available?" He waited a few moments for the captain to come on the line.

"Yes, Jones, what's up?"

"Cap, you're not going to believe this one!"

After explaining what they'd witnessed to his superior, he was told backup would soon arrive. Waiting together in the small office, staring at Peters' body through the window, Schneider suddenly cried, "What the hell is that?"

"What now?" Jones asked.

Joining his partner at the small window, he looked outside. They saw Peters' head slowly being jerked as if still alive. Then out of the skull crawled three small creatures resembling tarantulas. Their black bodies glistened in the sun as they crawled about the floor.

The creatures had bright red eyes, with a cornea and pupil resembling their host's eyes. All three had ten legs instead of the usual eight that arachnids have, and they displayed large fangs. One hissed, and venom jetted out. The trio joined at Peters' feet, making small screeching sounds to communicate.

Then, as if the dinner bell was rung, the other two scuttled over to two of the smoking corpses. One of the spider creatures, apparently the leader, raced up a body, displaying three long fangs that bit into one man's neck, feeding upon the remains of the man's blood. The other creatures crawled toward the other two bodies, and a feeding frenzy began. After several minutes the lone creature stopped and turned away from the pale corpse, having drunk the body clean of any blood.

As it paused its red pinchers danced about as if cleaning themselves. It suddenly froze in place and began to grow until it had doubled its size. It let out another screech as if calling to its companions. Its legs stretched out beyond its body; it continued to grow. Now the size of a cat, its menacing features were horrifying.

The other two spiders followed suit, one growing slightly larger than the other two. It tilted its head upward, tasting the air with its tiny black tongue. It called to the two creatures, and the trio joined and crawled toward the small office door.

Staring out from the protective window, Jones and Schneider watched helplessly as the creatures approached where they were hidden. The first creature appeared on the window, pausing upon the glass. It gawked at them, supported only by a strange substance secreted from its body, which smeared a yellowish coating across the glass. It crawled upward toward the roof and remained suspended, not moving. Its fangs tapped the glass, testing its strength.

Displaying his service revolver, Jones shouted out, "Get ready."

The spidery creature continued up the glass to the top of the door, then disappeared from view. The other two tarantulas followed.

Able to hear their movements above them, Jones nervously turned to his partner. "You don't think those creatures could get inside this office, do you?"

Never removing his eye from the ceiling, Schneider followed the clicking sounds as they crawled around the roof.

"I don't have a clue, but you better get ready. All I can say is that my skull will not be a nesting place for more of those creatures. I'd rather blow my brains out before allowing them to deposit their eggs in my head." Then he pointed his gun toward the sounds of the spider's movements.

Jones shook his head and said again, "I should have stayed home."

Chapter 12

STERLING SAT IN A FOLDING CHAIR at the back of the room as the Sleepy Hollow town meeting began. Several council members were seated behind a table overlooking the crowd. The discussion in the room centered around Stannis's sunken ship. However, that would have to wait as the mayor opened up the meeting with a long speech about the city's betterment. Another man spoke of a fundraiser at the orphanage this coming Saturday that all should attend.

The mayor then handed the meeting over to the town treasurer. An older woman in her seventies approached the overhead viewer with her graphs and charts. She explained how the city tax money was spent and how much of a shortfall the city would have the next fiscal year. Bored, Sterling stretched, letting out a tiresome yawn.

Twenty minutes had passed, and Sterling found himself trapped in an annoying fiscal hell with no end. The woman's voice began lulling him to sleep as he sat there. In his relaxed state Sterling heard a slight clapping of hands. Then another council member began speaking about Stannis's ship, asking for suggestions on what to do with the eyesore.

Sterling listened to people arguing. Some wanted to keep the wreck as a tourist attraction, exploiting the fact that a crown prince from Dubai once owned it. Anyone wishing to see the ship could pay a fee to see it rotting away.

A councilwoman at the end of the table suggested that it would be better to tear the old pier down, scrap the ship, and sell the land to a real estate developer who wants to build condos along the shorefront.

Sterling tried to make sense of each argument. Some had positive outcomes for the small town. Others were motivated by greed. His spirit began to be pricked with a strange feeling that he hadn't experienced since the incident with Tom Taylor. The sound of a little, faraway voice reached out to him. Almost familiar in some ways, it was yet strange and unnerving.

"Sterling, Sterling, my friend, please hear me."

The voice was familiar! He closed his mind to all influences and looked inward. The vision's obscurity cleared. A soft glow appeared. Before him lay a man on a granite table. Drawing closer, he studied the illusion. It was Stannis, though he looked much older than Sterling remembered.

He had no clue where he was. His psychic abilities, still weakened, waned, disconnected, and reconnected like a faulty telephone signal. Still, Sterling was excited. No matter how weak he still had his abilities, and Stannis had made himself known.

"Stannis," he whispered, not wanting anyone to hear him.

"Yes, I'm here but having difficulty reaching you from the spiritual realm," came the muffled response.

"Where are you, man?" Sterling asked but got no answer.

A few minutes later he heard the voice speak again. "Please listen. You cannot let my ship be boarded by anyone other than myself. Inside is the treasure that must be kept safe from mortal ne'er-do-wells. I was hoping you could buy my ship before they discover what's inside. Offer them two hundred and fifty large; that amount should make them lick their lips."

Sterling, hearing the request, wasn't sure how to respond. However, Stannis seemed to listen to his thoughts and replied, "I don't expect you to bankroll such a sizeable amount of money. Tell them you need a month to produce the full amount."

"I'm glad you have such grand ideas; I would not know where to begin such an adventure," Sterling said to himself after hearing the proposal.

"Sterling, please listen to me. All you have to do is translate the proposal to the town. Knowing their small-minded city government, they'll be happy to see my ship leave. Afterward, the town folk will undoubtedly thank you with many pats on your back. Now step up; it's time."

"Stannis, where are you? How do I find you? Please tell me! Where are you, man?" But his questions went unanswered. There was only silence.

Things became heated as the town's city council argued about the best possible course of action. After a brief pause, Sterling suddenly spoke aloud, drawing everyone's attention.

"I'd like to offer two hundred and fifty thousand dollars for the boat. I'll clear it from your docks. I only need a month to make the arrangements."

The room fell silent. The Beautification Committee had found someone who would charge the town twenty thousand dollars to move the wreck. Now someone was offering to pay to take it away.

There were smiles; Sterling received praise and

pats from people he had never met, including the mayor. Sterling silently shook his head and thought, *I don't want that piece of junk. Maybe this is Stannis's way of causing me grief for not staying in touch over the years.* Regardless, he was now the proud owner of one hundred tons of scrap.

After the meeting a slightly overweight woman in her thirties approached him. She wore jeans and cowboy boots, her lengthy hair in a braid under a cowboy hat, and said, "I'm Alexandra Sabine."

"Glad to meet you," Sterling responded, shaking her hand warmly.

The noisy room in the city hall was filled with conversations that mainly involved how the city would spend the two hundred and fifty thousand. Sterling, wanting to understand more about the battle between the two wizards, asked if they could find a quiet place to talk.

A smile appeared on Alexandra's face. "Follow me. I know a place."

Once outside the noise levels decreased noticeably. Walking down the sidewalk a short distance, they entered a pub, and Sterling followed Alexandra to the back and a booth near a window. After sitting down a waitress she knew arrived to take their orders, a tall Mai Tai for her and a scotch on the rocks for Sterling.

"I think you're the town hero. Offering to buy that hunk of scrap relieves many citizens who were unhappy at seeing the ship rotting away."

"Yeah, well, I just wanted to do my part," Sterling laughed. "But what I'd like to know from you is what you might have seen, or should I say what your grandmother might have seen, the night the ship sank."

"Please understand. I don't know you, and I don't

mean to disrespect you or your grandmother, but earlier today I encountered a young man handing out leaflets about the ship's removal. He told me that your Grandmother Aurelia had seen events that seemed strange to her the night it blew up. I heard she was the one who called the paramedics to save the ship's owner."

"Yes, the guy handing out leaflets, Mickey, is a real loser. He's unemployed and likes to drink a lot. I wouldn't trust anything he says."

"Yes, well, I might have frightened him a little."

"Why, what do you mean?"

"Well, how can I say this without sounding like a charlatan? I might have spoken out of line when I told him not to take any boat rides. I saw in his future a time when he was wearing a life jacket. The truth is I felt sorry for the guy and gave him fifty bucks to buy a lotto ticket."

"Why did you do that?" Alexandra asked.

"I saw him bumming money from his hard-working sister, and I told him his luck was about to change. Hopefully, if he hits it big, he will remember his sister working at the Fisherman's Wharf. Anywho, I was asking him about what happened to the ship's owner. He explained that your grandmother was the one who called the paramedics about the owner of the ship. When I asked Mickey where she lived, he told me she had died. That was all he knew."

"What are you saying, Sterling? You're psychic?"

Just then the waitress arrived. Setting their drinks down and seeing the two conversing, she turned and quietly disappeared.

"Sometimes I experience visions involving people who I know or, in the case of Mickey, who incite an emotional response. I responded by telling him what I saw. I felt obliged to tell him; whether or not he listens is totally up to him. Regardless, please tell me about the night your grandmother saved the ship's owner."

"I remember that night vividly. Sometime in the morning strange light flashes and crashing booms awakened my grandmother. I had gotten home earlier; truthfully, I was still sloshed. Grandma yelled at me to come see the strange things happening down by the pier. Unfortunately, I could not wake up. She told me that later. I looked out my bedroom window and saw two men fighting with one another, using strange weapons that sent out brilliant-looking colors that lit up the night sky. The guy dressed in a black cloak got the better hand, knocking the older man to the ground."

"His name is Stannis, the ship's owner."

"Yes, I believe you're right; my grandmother mentioned him. She told me later that she saw something else that night that she wanted me to keep secret.

"Now I realize what I'm about to say sounds foolish, but she told me that she saw the man dressed in black perform magic. She said he waved his book, creating a dark circular opening into another dimension. After defeating Stannis, as you called him, the man disappeared into the black hole."

"That does sound a little farfetched—unless you believe in that sort of thing. So can you tell me what hospital they took the ship's owner to?"

"I think my grandmother said it was Sacred Heart. I don't know; I have struggled to deal with her loss since she passed. It's painful to talk about her. I loved her so much."

"I'm familiar with the loss of a loved one. Recently,

a beautiful woman I loved dearly passed from an illness that robbed her of precious life many of us cherished. I feel for your loss."

Lifting her glass, Alexandra said aloud, "A toast to the ones we loved and lost. May the memories of their loving tenderness never be forgotten."

"Yes, well done, I'll toast to that," Sterling agreed.

After downing the contents of his glass, he called over the waitress and ordered another round.

The rest of the evening was spent hearing tales of when Alexandra was a little girl growing up in the sleepy town and how her mother abandoned her as a child. Her Grandmother Aurelia had raised her. She told Sterling that she was engaged once to a sailor. He went off to war and never returned. Another round was ordered as Sterling listened to her relive the most painful events. She seemed to feel comfortable sharing those personal occasions with him.

The following day Sterling awoke with a headache. He slowly sat up, his head swimming and remembering last night's drink fest. Alexandra knew how to party. This fact became apparent after the fifth round of drinks. He was simply no match. Realizing he'd had too much to drink, she offered him a place to sleep for the night. It was an offer he couldn't refuse, especially since she had taken his car keys, denying him the ability to search for a hotel to spend the night.

Slipping his pants on, he grabbed his shirt from the adjacent chair, loosely buttoning it. The morning rays of sunlight filtered through the silky curtains.

Standing in the doorway in her bathrobe, Alexandra looked at him and laughed aloud, "How would you like a cup of coffee?"

"I would love a cup of coffee, thank you."

A cat appeared purring at his feet as he tried to gain his senses. "What's your name?" he asked, picking up the cat and gently petting it.

"His name is Bad—Bad to the bone," Alexandra chuckled. "Mostly, I just call him Bad."

"What an unlikely name for a cat."

"No, not really; he's an alley cat. Believe me, I've seen him in fights with another feline, and he always comes out the victor."

Laughing aloud, Sterling held the cat in his hands. "Is that true, Bad? Are you a badass?"

"He doesn't like strangers normally."

"I'm a cat lover. At home I have an old cat named Mr. Bigglesworth."

"And you said Bad was an odd name for a cat. That's funny, Sterling. Now tell me how you like your eggs?"

"Alexandra, please listen; you needn't make me breakfast, too. The hospitality you have shown by allowing me to use your couch is more than I would ever expect from anyone."

"It doesn't matter; I'm making breakfast. I'd rather share a meal with the company I enjoy than sit alone. So what will it be?"

Sterling suggested that he help.

"Sorry, pal. In this kitchen there is only one chef. Help yourself to a cup of coffee; the cups are in the cupboard beside you. The cream and sugar are on the table."

Over breakfast the conversation was pleasant. No discussions about lost loved ones. When Sterling finished his breakfast, he asked Alexandra if it would be alright to shower. He told her afterward he had some errands to run.

"Mi casa es su casa."

He left the second-story apartment above a hardware store, walked to his car parked on the road, and returned with his overnight bag. Within the hour he was showered and dressed.

The next order of business was to find Stannis. He knew he had to find a quiet place to meditate. He asked if he could be alone in a park or a peaceful place. Alexandra told him about a secluded city park with tall trees and green grass just out of town.

As Sterling was about to leave, he hugged Alexandra warmly, thanking her for the hospitality. Grabbing hold of the doorknob, he turned it slowly. Sterling felt a bizarre intimacy toward this woman he had known for less than a day. With strange bewilderment he couldn't explain, he knew she was a missing puzzle piece he had been searching for or would become someone needed in the future. The whole thing did not make any sense. There was no answer for the way he was feeling—none that he could explain.

Ignoring his feelings, he started to leave.

"You're that psychic who helped save that teenage girl many years ago, right?"

"What makes you say that?" Starling answered, turning back around.

"Ever since I was a little girl my Grandmother Aurelia talked about that kidnapping and would frighten me with stories of why I shouldn't talk to a stranger or else that could happen to me. She also told me girls were kidnapped so some old wizard could sacrifice them. She often told me that magic is real, not make-believe. I know that powerful magic was performed here in our small community. The man who owned the ship was a powerful sorcerer. The one who defeated him was even more powerful. Stannis's name is well known in certain circles involving the occult."

"How could you possibly know any of this?" Sterling asked.

"It's simple. Grandma Aurelia was an enchantress who performed magic. She is the only reason your friend Stannis survived."

Sterling turned back around, closing the door. His expression was of wonder and amazement. *What does that make you?* he thought.

Chapter 13

Deep down within a hidden tunnel, the tiny creature resembling a giant spider made its way toward an unknown location. Called to obey, it scampered through an old air vent down through cracks in the rock. Traversing through the rugged terrain was difficult. However, soon the creature arrived at an opening above a cave. Descending from a single greenish thread, it lowered itself into a room.

Black smoke billowed up into a hole in the ceiling. Inside the cave stood Tom Taylor performing a spell and working above a boiling cauldron. He had ingredients in his hands that he was about to deposit into the hot steaming liquid.

"Tras, Yuta, Cantic," he spoke aloud after depositing a handful of elements into the mixture. Instantly, this added solution caused the boiling liquid to cool, turning it red.

He sensed the appearance of the small black creature, and a grin appeared on his face. Tom looked up, seeing his small pet hanging from the ceiling. He casually walked over and reached out for his arachnid. Moving downward, it traveled the short distance, resting in Tom's hand.

The little monster quickly detected the rapid pumping of Tom's blood through his carotid arteries. It had fed earlier on the body of Sergeant Peters but had used up its energy to travel and was now hungry again. Tom held it loosely, and it began crawling up his arm, resting around its creator's neck.

Tom ignored his spider's hunger. He had bigger plans for his little scamper. Walking back, he reached up to the top shelf. He removed a pinch of bats' hearts from a small canister. Combining it with snake eyes and the bladder of an alligator, he crushed them together in a small stone bowl. Reaching for cyanide powder from a cassava shrub, he dropped the contents in the pot.

As he stirred the deadly mixture slowly, Tom spoke an enchantment, "Babbo, Issiaca, Tarnuke."

Black smoke erupted outward, turning the liquid a bright blue color, then back to red. He dropped the final ingredients inside his black pot.

Taking a sharp knife, he placed his hand over the mixture and sliced it across his palm. Immediately, blood began to pour down into the liquid. Tom could hear his little monster dancing about excitedly, smelling the blood in the air. Taking a spoon, he dipped it into the liquefied batch to fill, reached for a glass bottle, and slowly filled the magical potion inside. Holding the decanter aloft, he watched the fluid turn different colors as its components combined. Finally, it turned lime green.

He reached up, took hold of his creature, and lowered it to the floor. It moved excitedly about as it felt the magical essence in the room. It knew that changes would happen as Tom approached. It froze in place, unmoving, connected through telepathy to its master. The spider would obey Tom's every command.

Waving his hand, he motioned for the creature to turn on its back, exposing its belly. There, made visible to only him, was a green hourglass image. Its deadly, poisonous bite would be fatal to anyone. However, Tom had other plans, more sinister in design.

Kneeling, he poured the magical potion on the spider's underbelly. Once the entire contents had been poured, he stepped back. The spider squealed in pain. Its legs jerked outward. Its body began to split apart, growing larger and larger. Greenish liquid dripped onto the marble floor, sending off toxic-looking smoke.

The creature, who had been no larger than a hamster, doubled in size repeatedly. Its cries changed from tiny shrieks to deep-sounding moans. Now the size of a dog, the legs broke off and were discarded; they lay on the ground next to the body as their nerves sent off spasms, jerking wildly.

The body grew outward, changing colors from jet-black to gray to red. The abdomen continued to pull apart, stretching beyond its capacity. Small appendages appeared on the body. Its head increased in size as well. A pronounced jawline grew outward. Its eight eyes turned purple, with thick veins of yellowish liquid pulsating across the eyeballs.

Tom watched as it began to crawl. It had only traveled a short distance, anxious to feel its ever-powerful body. Silky, red hairs started to cover its body from its head to the end of its round shape. Still developing, it grew new legs that were powerful and robust; its body became muscular.

Now the size of a calf, its legs extended under its body, supporting its weight. A long, slippery tongue jetted out of the creature's mouth, licking the air. Four sets of large green eyes appeared. Opening and looking about, it saw its master. It shrugged its head side to side, making wheezing sounds through its ever-expanding lungs.

It continued to get bigger, becoming the size of a full-grown cow. Large claws extended from its feet; they made clicking noises on the hard floor as its nails grew. Sharp-looking fags grew out of its jaws. The creature's head was now quite large and hairy. Soon it had large pointy ears extending out of its skull that twitched as it began hearing sounds never known.

As it continued to grow, its body became astoundingly unique. Never throughout evolution had anything such as this existed. Stepping back, Tom couldn't have been more pleased.

The beast stood on its rear legs. Now the size of a large adult polar bear, it stood over twelve feet, weighing nearly three thousand pounds. It opened its mouth and bellowed out a roar.

Tom approached the beast. It lowered its head and felt the sorcerer's touch.

As Tom began to pet his creature, he said, "Now it is time that you take your place in the other dimension as a protector elect of my book of magic. Anyone tempted to open or steal the book's secrets will be destroyed."

The shaking of its head meant that it understood its purpose in life. The creature smelled the blood that still dripped from Tom's hand. Its slippery tongue stretched outward toward his hand and began to lick the red liquid.

Something peculiar happened as it tasted blood for the first time: The monster became invisible. Tom stood there, focused on the creature, but it had vanished entirely before his eyes. Yet, he could still see his creation next to him in a mirror. His pet had the ability to project its image into other dimensions or vanish from sight.

A few minutes later it changed back again. Seeing these strange abilities brought Tom unimaginable joy.

He stared at his creation and said, "Soon, beast, you shall have your fill of blood; be patient, my pet." Tom glanced at his wound; the pain was no longer there. Something about the way the animal's saliva mixed with his blood caused the cut to begin to close, turning a blue color. Each of his fingers suddenly glowed. A fiery line connected each of his digits, then the incision disappeared.

The reality of what he was seeing pleased him very much. Not only was his beast a killing machine but it also was enabled with magical abilities to heal him.

After setting the empty bottle on the shelf over the cauldron, Tom picked up an old magic book. He slowly turned the pages as if looking for something in particular, perhaps a spell he had once seen. All manner of possibilities existed here within these very pages. One could curse a loved one, causing an excruciating death. There was also a spell to change the will of powerful men, such as kings or nobles.

The curse that created the Jillian Dagger was there as well. Wealth and prestige: He had all he wanted. A long life was his already, promised by the dark lord himself. Now he looked for something else in particular.

He was distracted by the monstrous beast prowling around the room. He set the book down to gather his thoughts. He considered the rocky cave he was standing in. This secret place had once belonged to Tobias. Abandoned for over a hundred years, no one ventured down its dark passageways. It was thought to be haunted, which was to Tom's liking.

Since the dark lord Tobias had enchanted him, Tom

knew its many secrets, including Tobias's dwelling where he had worked his magic, controlling mortals like Tom's own father, Martin. The latter was defenseless against such a powerful spell. Then Tom thought of Eileen, his stepmother, and how she suffered under Tobias's abuse. A smile appeared, thinking of her suffering.

In another room candles sent an eerie glow into the cavern. Here underground was a medieval device that looked like a throne of sorts. Its outer structure was made from human bones and held together with strands of pure silver. Its base was decorated with human skulls piled up to the armrests. The seat was made from human skin that was stretched and sewn in place with gold thread. The back of the chair displayed a shield made of pure gold. The image carved on the shield was a pentagram rising above a moon. Underneath was a turbulent sea crashing upon a rocky shoreline.

Nearby were two standing tripods with sharp, spear-like blades that pointed toward one another. In the center, supported by the knives, was a crystal ball. Its black polished surface reflected the room's image. Now, absent of life or powerful magic, it slept until it would awaken to do its master's calling.

As a gift from his dark master, Tom had been presented with an accomplice, a demon name Drasidan. He was given the power to persuade the minds of the parole board to set Tom free from prison.

Initially, when given the mark upon his hand, he thought his role in life was to perform a sacrifice that Tobias could not complete. However, when the demon appeared to him in prison, he was told to be an instrument in the dark lord's design to bring about the Apocalypse, the end of humanity.

Within eight days of that first meeting, Tom was a free man. Since then Drasidan has continued to assist him in learning the skills needed to perform magic. After all, what was magic except a pinch of evil powers being ignited? Now imagine the whole collection at your disposal.

Tom was ordered to have a showdown with Stannis to test his skills, taking him to the domain of evil that the dark lord controlled. Stannis was a nuisance who had to be brought down and destroyed. Defeating Stannis would prove his worthiness.

Giving all his mortal being to studying the black arts, Tom was prepared to wage war on the unsuspecting wizard. Precisely at midnight he had appeared at Stannis's abode. The sensation of another worker of magic so close in proximity caused the old necromancer to crawl out of his shelter, prepared for battle. They soon fought for supremacy. However, with renewed power given by the demon Drasidan, Tom sent bolts of powerful magic directly at Stannis's armor. Ultimately, he cast a spell to grasp the man's heart, ensuring death.

The second book of magic once belonged to Tobias. It was something that Tom had wanted above all else. He knew that Stannis had once held it in his possession, and only Stannis knew where it was. Gladly, he defeated the older man and sent him to hell. Still, he did not have Tobias's second book—the one with the spell to place his creature inside his book to protect it. Perhaps there, under the waves of that Stannis's sunken ship, is where the book was.

I must find it, Tom thought.

Looking at his monster, Tom knew that it must soon eat. *What better place to find a meal than a Bishop's residence? Wait until the dark lord sees you; won't he be proud?*

Above the ceiling three shapes appeared, lowering themselves into the room from a single thread spun from their bodies.

"I see that you have hatched from your confines. Be ready for I have great plans for you and my pets," Tom said, looking at the creatures. A deep, jubilant laugh erupted from him. It echoed in the small place and rocked the timbers as the ground shook from the powerful force of dark magic.

Chapter 14

HE PARKED HIS CAR AT A PARTICULAR address and walked to the house. He paused for a moment at the front door. After pressing the doorbell he waited for the inhabitants to answer the door. A few moments later the homeowner peeked through the sidelight. He heard the deadbolt unlock; the door swung open. Upon seeing Jacob on the door's other side, Rachel knew he was there to tell her that her father had been found.

"Just tell me if he's alive."

"I'm so sorry, Rachel."

"No, it can't be. Oh my god, how can I tell Melissa that Dad is gone?" she cried, collapsing on her knees and weeping bitterly.

"Rachel, please listen. Nothing could be done for your father. He is now at peace. I came here first because I thought it best for Melissa to hear the news from someone she trusts rather than a stranger. I don't believe Melissa could handle the news in her delicate condition. You've always been the strong one in the family."

"Damn it, Jacob, you can't be referring to her past drug abuse. It's not my sister's fault that she used drugs to cope with the nightmarish things she had to endure. How in hell would you have dealt with it being the target of a murder plot at age sixteen?" Rachel responded, wiping the tears away.

"Rachel, please listen to me. I thought of nothing but your family when I got the call from the coroner's office confirming your father's remains."

"My father's remains? No, it can't be, Jacob. Do you hear me? It can't be."

Kneeling, Jacob grabbed hold of Rachel as she was flooded with emotion, childhood memories, and her love for her father. Now hearing that he was gone seemed like the beginning of a nightmare from which she would never wake up. When would her family ever be free from the misery of losing the ones they loved?

Time no longer means anything when one discovers a loved one has passed and the time for mourning has begun. Pulling free of Jacob's tender embrace, Rachel stood to her feet and disappeared inside her house to retrieve some tissues. She returned and, wiping her eyes, said, "Could you please tell me: Do you believe my father suffered?"

"I can't tell you that," he said, looking down at his feet. "I'm not an expert on such things, but an official report from the coroner's office will describe such details. Please, listen to me. I'm not sure you really want to know any of that."

"Why wouldn't I?"

He paused and thought, *I described it best when I said that Rachel was the most influential member of the family. She never deserted her sister during her drug use. No, not even when family valuables, such as her mother's prized diamond earrings and a gold brooch, went missing. She alone survived, going through the attempted sacrifice unchanged.*

However, the most disturbing thought was the loss of the once prized crystal object that was critical in saving them from the powerful wizard. Jacob had firsthand knowledge of how powerful it had been. He grabbed his throat reflexively, still feeling the sensation of being strangled. The nightmarish memories never left him.

"All I'm saying is that for now maybe you don't want to know such details. Instead, think about your sister and how you will tell her the bad news."

"Perhaps you're right; nothing can be done for now. Still, I don't care, Jacob. You need to find Tom Taylor. I can tell you this, none of us are safe—not anyone! That man has it in his mind to kill us all!"

"You have to believe me when I say we're doing everything possible to find him. It's as if he disappeared from the face of the planet."

"All right, thank you for coming here to tell me about my father. We'll arrange his burial together when I can develop the courage to tell Melissa."

"You have my number?"

"Yes, I still have you on speed dial."

"If you can think of anything that you might need, don't hesitate to call me."

"I will. You have my word."

"I'm sorry for your loss; I always liked your father."

"Yes, he had a way with people. Thank you again, Jacob."

After Rachel closed the door, Jacob returned to his unmarked police vehicle. He lit a cigarette before reporting to dispatch. Sitting alone in his squad car, he thought of his job in law enforcement. This part of the job was the worst. He hated giving bad news to loved ones. Yes, it was a portion of the job but still, it sucked.

When he finished his cigarette, he deposited it in

the ashtray. Grabbing the mic, he reported to dispatch. He was told to report to the chief. Speeding away, Jacob drove back to the station.

Unknown to Rachel or Jacob, eyes watched their encounter with renewed interest.

"It looks like the bitch got the news about her father," Samantha boasted.

Sitting in the driver's seat on the corner across the street, Aaliyah responded, "Yes, won't our master be pleased."

"Oh, wait a minute. I just felt my baby kick for the first time."

Aaliyah ignored the statement and drove away. Leaving the small neighborhood, they pulled out onto a busy intersection, heading downtown.

Looking over at her passenger, Aaliyah responded, "I have felt my baby kicking the shit out of me for these past two weeks. I'm so proud to bring to life the master's legacies. When he rises to power, we will have a place of honor among the common people and be worshipped as gods."

"A god—think about it! My damn mother thought I would never amount to anything. Just look at me now."

"Tom Taylor—it is he who we must please. It's not his fault that the genes of the Taylor family are cursed with a rare disease that kills infants every other generation."

Samantha, wearing a smile, said, "I wonder if Master Taylor will want us to send another bouquet of black roses to the Bishop woman's home?"

"I'm not sure."

"I liked what you wrote in that little card when their mother died. There is something that I have always wanted to ask you. Clever, very clever, I must say! How exactly did you come up with that message?" Samantha asked.

"Back in Brazil I used to be a writer."

"A writer; I could never be someone that gifted. I was born with a golden spoon in my mouth. No talent there."

"No, not talent for me. Just utter frustration. Being a successful writer means hard work and luck. As the rejections started to pile up, so did my anger. One day I had enough and decided to end my life. I had consumed a bottle of Tequila and thought that the best way to die was to hang myself. Alone on my balcony, I took some rope and tied a noose around my neck."

"Hang yourself? Really?"

"Yes, at the time it sounded like an answer to all my problems," Aaliyah explained.

Samantha looked out the window at the busy streets. "I just did a drug overdose. Got high and touched the stars," she said.

"That works, too, I suppose. Anyway, I was lying there dying, with the rope around my neck strangling me. I was visited by the demon Drasidan, who offered me a new life as a Taylor mother. I accepted his offer and was spared certain death. A short time later I met Tom."

"That sounds cool, almost love at first sight. right?"

"The demon monitored me. When I was ovulating I was taken to Tom. As we kissed, he said something that I won't ever forget. He told me that the smell of death was still on my body. This odor aroused him; we made love for hours," Aaliyah explained.

"I, too, had a unique experience, although not as glamorous as yours. I had a drug overdose, and Drasidan visited me. However, the only scent I smelled of was vomit."

Both women laughed together, seeing the rather macabre humor in Samantha's story.

After arriving at the expensive condo, they parked the BMW in the garage. They rode up to the penthouse apartment purchased with Samantha's inheritance. Once inside they were greeted by Aeneas, Tom's albino protégé.

"I understand that both the Bishop daughters have been informed of their father's death?" he asked.

"Yes, it is true, as the master ordered it," Aaliyah expounded.

"Very well. Won't the Bishops be surprised when the rest of their father's body arrives?"

"What do you mean, Aeneas?" Samantha asked.

He walked over to two granite boxes, each a jet-black color. Both boxes were the size of a shoebox. On the outside were symbols, like the stone used in the father's sacrifice. Aeneas touched one of the lids, careful not to open the contents. He turned back and smiled.

"A hand from the woman's father is now placed inside each box," he announced.

"For what purpose?" Aaliyah inquired.

"A trap. It's a trap. Once the box is opened, a horrible living creature that the master has created will be magically transported to the box to kill and eat those living mortals not protected by the sign," he explained.

"That's brilliant. Master is so clever," Aaliyah proclaimed.

"Can you hear me, beast? Be patient. Soon you'll be eating to your heart's content," Samantha announced while tracing the edge of a lid with her finger and wearing a sinister smile.

An unexpected sensation of pure evil shot out from the box's confines, overwhelming her senses and causing the child within her womb to kick her as if it were connected magically to the evil force inside.

Laughing hysterically, Samantha said, "I need a drink."

The women were about to leave the room when Aeneas warned sternly, "Listen to me carefully. The twins born of the Bishop bloodline—if anything happens to them, you will wish you had never been born."

Boldly, Aaliyah stepped forward; her expression changed as she spoke. "Nothing will ever happen to us; we're the mothers of our lord's seed!"

Aeneas's gaze was fixated as he pointed his finger at both women. "Hear what I'm saying to you; Neither of you will be spared if one Bishop twin dies. You have been warned!"

Samantha pointed her finger back at Aeneas. "Listen to me, cowboy, Aaliyah and I have spread our legs to bear your master his kids. Now do not forget to whom you're talking. We outrank you here, dumbass. In the end when Tom Taylor is ruling the world, you'll be lucky if I don't make you a shoeshine boy or, worse yet, a worker at the sewage plant,"

Ignoring Samantha's outburst, Aeneas stepped toward her menacingly. "I have a question for both of you. Answer me: Do you not understand that I have studied dark magic my entire life? Even now I could create a spell that would place a wart on your noses so large it would disgust my master, Taylor! You'd repulse him. Your bodies look plump and overweight. Have you ever considered why my master hasn't been to visit you in many nights? You both have one purpose: to bring into this world and deliver offspring worthy to inherit this planet. Nothing more. You spread your legs like a twenty-dollar whore who walks the streets at night. Are you whores then?"

After a moment of silence, Samantha shouted, "I need a drink,"

"No, not a drink for already your weakness with alcohol is known to the demon Drasidan and me. Be careful. Heed my warning, both of you. There is powerful magic at work that neither of you realizes. You have been warned, you self-proclaimed bitches."

Chapter 15

STERLING ASKED, "WHAT DOES that make you?"

Alexandra answered, "I'm gifted with a unique power to interrupt evil, to discover its weaknesses, and at times offer to heal from the effects. As I said, my Grandmother Aurelia was an enchantress. Since my youth I have been raised to understand magic. Magic!" She laughed. "It's such a simple word; let me say this instead. I was raised to comprehend forces at work of a unique nature, especially when it comes to the effects of dark magic on the populace such as serial killers and rapists."

"I'm a clairvoyant. I, too, am gifted with certain abilities that allow me to see into the future or past to experience events for which there are no explanations."

"Am I out of line when I say that perhaps we two should join forces?" Alexandra asked.

Sterling closed the door, walked back into the apartment, and sat on the sofa. A moment late, he responded, "The honest truth is that I don't work well with others. I'm a lone wolf."

"A lone wolf, huh? All I'm saying is that I may not be a wolf but I can be a bitch at times. I believe that we'll get along just fine." She laughed again.

"You're a gusty broad; I like you. I already see a toughness within you that is very pleasing. However, I must tell you that in battles previously fought I have seen loved ones fall to powers unexplainable; this could happen here. I don't want to feel responsible for another death."

"Sterling, you can really be melodramatic at times. Has anyone ever told you that?"

"Yes, once. Someone to whom I gave my heart. She knew me like no one else. I lost her, unable to save her life. I helplessly watched as she took her last breath."

A chink in the armor of the man presented itself. Seeing this made Alexandra like Sterling even more. He was not an arrogant man—like many he had met in the past. *Conceit, heck, who needs it?* she thought. Those types of men could never accept her telling them the truth.

Sterling's expression changed as if the pain of his loss was a burden that wounded him gravely.

"Sterling, listen to me. I'm not from your past and don't expect to suffer from an unwanted illness. My life is meant for greatness, a sign in the stars. I have been granted unique abilities. No, I'm not a powerful sorceress, but what I can do is heal. The pain that you're suffering from does not involve magic of any sort. It's a part of life; we are born and die. There is nothing magical about it, although some have tried to escape it over the centuries by using magic."

"Alexandra, I see you're strong and compassionate. Of course, I want your help," Sterling answered.

"I suppose that the first order of business is to find your friend Stannis, the conjurer who disappeared."

"Yes, I've already been contacted by Stannis telepathically. Strangely, I'm not sure if he is still alive or speaking to me from the great beyond. Since I was struck by an unknown force back in my apartment, nothing seems clear to me anymore, although just a short time ago I felt compelled to be your friend. You are key. To what I don't know, but you are crucial."

"I see a need that has arisen so I will respond; that's the type of person I am. Yes, I, too, have felt the fellowship you speak. Sterling, call it fate if you wish but somehow a woman always knows."

"Knows what exactly?"

"Sterling, you're damaged goods."

"Oh really. Well, thank you very much."

"You're quite welcome. Why are we still standing here, Sterling? We should have started this journey to the unknown. It's past the time."

"My car is warming up as we speak. I'm waiting for you."

"No, you're not; I only need a few minutes to throw something on. I'll be back in two shakes of a lamb's tail." Then Alexandra quickly disappeared into her bedroom.

Sterling walked over to look out the second-floor window. Staring at the sunken ship, he saw a strange light emitting from the depths of the vessel past the command bridge, down into the bowels of the hull.

Just then Alexandra appeared. After grabbing her bag she pushed Sterling out the front door of her apartment and onto the second-floor deck, then stopped short, remembering something. She paused and said, "Wait, I'll be right back."

She glanced around her comfortable apartment and headed outside. After walking back inside, she went to her bedroom. There, inside an antique armoire, were all kinds of odd-looking trinkets. After removing a key from a hidden compartment on the floor, she unlocked a drawer in the chest and pulled it open. After pulling out two small stones, she dropped them into her purse and locked the drawer tight.

She felt sad about leaving her home. Would she ever see it again? She took her house keys and locked the deadbolt into place. She followed Sterling to his car, got inside, and they drove away.

Driving up the interstate to reach the hospital where Aurelia said they had taken the powerful wizard took several hours. On the way Sterling brought up Alexandra's last statement.

"All right, now that we're 'friends.' The air quotes were evident in the way he said the word. "Tell me, please, what did you mean by saying I'm damaged goods? Damn it, I barely know you, and yet you can easily make that observation about my character?"

"Sterling, you're a nice enough guy. I like you, really, I do. But what haunts you I cannot fix. It's not up to me but up to her!"

"Her?" Sterling responded.

"Yes, Sterling, I'm not your soulmate or else I would feel it. Last night you would not have slept on the hard couch alone if I'd known you were the one for me. Life is too short for us mortal humans. To find true love is the rarest of all things we endure in life."

"Alexandra, I had a vision. I have seen her, the woman you speak of. Down to my very soul I believe that what you are saying is true. I caught a glimpse of her and the children. Damn it, hear me. I can't be sure if what I saw is real."

"Sterling, you're a psychic, right? Why would you doubt?"

Sterling shook his head. "There are facts about me I have not shared with you. My clairvoyant capacities have been altered; they are nothing now."

"Altered how?"

"Does the name Tom Taylor mean anything to you?"

"Tom Taylor, the serial killer that went to prison years ago?"

"The same. I'm one of the ones that sent Tom there. He hasn't forgotten what I did."

"Oh, I see."

"Look, we're here," Sterling said, ending the conversation. He felt relieved. It had become entirely too uncomfortable. After parking the car, he turned to Alexandra.

"Listen, all I'm saying is that I believe this Tom has performed a spell on me that blocks my telepathic abilities. That makes me uncertain of the vision I saw. Part of me wants to believe that there is someone for me who will love me unconditionally. Still, I have doubts. You don't know what this bastard is capable of doing. The world doesn't know but will soon be awakened as a prisoner of his imagination and powerful magic."

"If what my Grandmother Aurelia has told me is true, all of us are in for a battle. Look, Sterling, I cannot say if you will ever find true love, the love you are speaking of. But sometimes we spend so much time searching for that special person that we discount the ones standing before us."

"Again, I know you are right, but here is the strangest thing. In my vision I heard someone call out her name—a waiter handing her the drink bill. There, in paradise, she waits for me. If I spend the rest of my life waiting and hoping, I will be the biggest fool above everyone else on this miserable planet."

"A fool in search of love? Aren't we all at times, Sterling?"

"Yes, indeed."

"Before we go inside, I have just one more question. Her name, tell me the name of the woman in your vision. Who knows? Perhaps I know her."

"Her name? That's the damnedest thing, Alexandra. In my vision I didn't hear her name. You would think my psychic abilities would let me know, but they don't. I know only her last name and will not tell you. I'm sorry. I don't know what's gotten into me. It's as if when she's discovered, all my walls will be torn down, exposing my weaknesses with no defenses left for me so all I can do is surrender. More than that, much more, the future is unknown to me. We together, no longer two separate lives; ours will be intertwingled. What does that mean? Is it possible I will go forward using my psychic abilities or will I give this talking to the dead stuff a proper burial? You ask me for a name I will not tell you. But know this: The day I find her my world will be forever changed. I cannot talk about it further. I feel emotional when I do. Please forgive me."

"Now I see. Now I understand the depth of your desires, Sterling. Please do not tell me her name; we will allow fate to play its part."

"Good. Alexandra, you see what a great friend you have become to me already."

"I do. The feeling is shared. Let's go in and find your friend Stannis."

"You got it, babe."

"Hm, Sterling, are you sure you wouldn't rather tell me her name? You should know this sort of thing drives a woman crazy."

"Alexandra, really?"

"I'm just kidding." Alexandra laughed at him.

"Okay, but somehow I know you're not letting this

go lightly."

After grabbing her arm, they walked into the hospital and up to an older woman sitting at a desk. He asked to see Stannis, not knowing any name or other identifying information; it was the only name he knew for him.

The woman looked up the name on her computer and said, "Oh, dear, I'm afraid Mr. Stannis has passed away!"

Chapter 16

JACOB READ THE CRIME LAB results carefully, particularly noting the substance discovered in the body's remains. A caustic acid had been found both inside the skull and torso. The two homicide detectives that worked the case, Schneider and Jones, were familiar to him. Still, he wanted to understand better why the report described such imaginative details.

The bizarre was nothing new to him; he had seen what the dark wizard Tobias had done. It still haunted his dreams. He shrugged off the memories. It was late, and most detectives had left for the day. Hoping to find Jones or Schneider still working, Jacob walked to where the homicide department was located. When he arrived Schneider was seated at his desk, staring at a cold cup of coffee. No one spoke to him or acknowledged his existence but did their jobs as if he weren't there.

Jacob didn't move to see who stood there when he appeared beside his desk. He had bags under his eyes, and his face wore a dark five o'clock shadow. He looked as if he hadn't slept in days.

"Detective Schneider, do you have a minute?"

"Yeah, what do you need?"

"My name is Detective Marks. I reviewed your report concerning the body you and your partner found at the Whisper Pines resort in the Catskills Mountains.

You and your partner have not agreed on some conflicting details."

"My partner," Schneider whispered.

"Hey buddy, are you feeling okay?" Jacob asked.

The man kept repeating, "My partner."

Jacob didn't know what he should do, if anything. Looking around the room, no one seemed to notice their conversation. However, Jacob realized this wasn't the place to discuss the supernatural.

"Hey, let's get out of here; I know a good place to talk alone. I want to discuss something with you that I believe you will find most interesting," Jacob said, looking down at the man.

"Sure, whatever you say."

Standing to his feet, Schneider took his coat from the back of the chair. Following Jacob out to his police cruiser, they drove to a bar known by most of the cops. On the way there neither one spoke. After pulling around back, Jacob parked. Inside they sat in an empty booth at the back. A waitress Jacob was familiar with, Peggie, approached and took their order.

Once the coffee arrived Jacob watched Schneider lift his cup to take a drink. The man acted dazed. From all accounts the guy's nerves were shot. He'd received many accomplishments and accolades for heroism, but now he was shaken. After finishing his cup of coffee, he quietly stared out into space.

Wanting to break the ice, Jacob asked, "Did you ever hear of the Bishop kidnapping?"

His immediate response was, "Yeah, what about it?"

"I'm the guy that drove the milk truck."

"What milk truck?"

"The one in which Tom Taylor made his escape.

I thought that you said you remembered the case?"

"Hey, listen, that was years ago, all right!" Standing to leave, Schneider turned back and said, "Thanks for the coffee."

Before he took another step, Jacob said, "I know what you're going through. I know about the nightmares as well."

Schneider froze and didn't move. "Nightmares?"

"Yes, that's what I said, the damn nightmares."

After sitting back down, Schneider whistled for the waitress to come over and ordered a Scotch. "The nightmares are the worst."

"You don't have to tell me; I remember them all too well."

Just then the waitress appeared with Schneider's drink. Staring at Jacob, she asked if he would care for something more substantial than coffee.

"Sure, why not? I'm off the clock in twenty minutes. I'll take a whiskey straight up."

Schneider took the glass and emptied it in a single motion before Peggie had a chance to leave. He asked for another.

"What gets me is the nightmares and how they have affected my partner. The guy hasn't returned to work since we were trapped in the old resort."

Jacob leaned closer. "What exactly happened at the Whisper Pines resort? I read your reports, but they conflict."

Schneider's face was white as a sheet as he mumbled, "It was spiders, but not any spiders you or anyone else has ever seen. Shit, no, not in your wildest imagination could you ever dream up something as horrifying as these creatures."

"Tell me what happened. How did you escape?"

"We never did escape! I see them every night when I close my eyes."

"What happened to your partner? Surely, Jones wasn't bitten or anything, was he?"

"No, neither of us was bitten, but we were standing behind a door in the kitchen pantry. I told Jones to pull his service revolver and be prepared for battle. Honestly, I thought the two of us were goners."

"How? Why?"

Staring intently into the distance, Schneider explained, "We watched the damn creatures attack three men and suck their blood. We stood helpless as these creatures were hatched from the human remains of one man, and afterward, they began to grow. What started out the size of a small tarantula suddenly grew much larger—the size of a cat, and then they crawled up the wall and ended up on the roof above Jones and me."

"They walked straight up the walls?"

"Listen to me. As I said, we thought we were both goners; we could hear their little legs scurrying upon the roof and across to the other side, then nothing at all. We weren't sure if they had found a way inside the kitchen area and we would be their next meal."

"Tell me, what happened next?"

"Well, we saw our chance to get away and took it. We ran out that door, pointing our guns at anything that moved. After jumping into our police cruiser, we tore out of Dodge and didn't look back. Now the only question is: Are we a forgotten memory or at any time could the spiders appear to suck our blood?"

"Alright, Schneider, please listen to me. I have survived being choked to death by a creature that couldn't be explained, whose strength was unreal. There was a battle raging, and I can tell you who was behind it: Tom Taylor. He alone has been granted some special powers from the devil to perform these unhuman things. I have been searching for him, but he eludes me."

Just then Peggie appeared carrying the next rounds of drinks, set them down, and left.

"What about Jones? He's a married man with a family."

"I suggest that we visit him. I want to hear his side of the events you described."

"Why are we waiting? Come on. I'll show you where he lives. I know he'll be awake. I doubt he can sleep," Schneider said, emptying his glass.

Jacob paid the bill and left a sizeable tip. Soon he would get to the bottom of what happened at Whisper Pines. It seemed that, once again, it was a place where evil resided.

On the way to Jones' house, Schneider talked of the different cases he and his partner had worked together in homicide. He even mentioned a name that was familiar to Detective Marks: Sterling.

"So you know Sterling?"

"Yes, I've met him only once when Jones and I worked the Harper case. Rayleen Harper's body was found five miles away in the trunk of an abandoned car near Memorial Park."

"I used to go swimming there."

"A drainage ditch ran toward the back of the park where kids like to park to make out. That was where Sterling told us to start looking."

"Did you ever find the killer?"

"As a matter of fact, we did. Steve Watson was once Tom Taylor's cellmate. It seems that Tom suggested that by offering him the heart of a virgin girl, Steve would have riches and a long life. Shit, who doesn't want that, right?"

"Tom Taylor. Whoever would have thought that the greedy little bastard could grow up to become such a murderer? Sure, the guy was motivated by money, but now it seems it is just death and destruction. By the way, he disemboweled Mark Harding—carved him up like a turkey. Tom is the man responsible. All I have to do is find him."

The pair pulled up to Jones' house. The outside lights shone brightly out into the street. All the lamps were on, revealing a living room with a couch against the wall. A family portrait could be seen hanging above the fireplace through the sheer curtains

The men walked up the narrow sidewalk to the front door and knocked softly.

Someone peered out the curtains and said, "Yes, can I help you?"

"Jones, open the door. It's me."

"Yeah, sure, but who is the guy with you?"

"He's Detective Marks, working with missing persons. Open the door before we disturb your family."

Slowly, the door creaked open. Standing on the other side was Jones. His hair was uncombed; he wore a dirty shirt that hung outside his pants, dirty white socks, and no shoes.

"My family isn't here; they left me—all three children, including my wife. I came home from work one day. They were gone, can you believe it?" he mumbled.

"When did this happen?" Schneider asked.

"Over a week ago, I suppose."

"Hey, listen to me. Detective Marks understands what we've gone through; he had been involved in the missing person case about twenty years ago when he tried to help the famous Tom Taylor escape."

"Wait a damn minute! That happened a long time ago! I'm now a detective; you can't judge me for something I did when I was young and dumb," Jacob argued.

"Look at us. We're not very young, but I suppose you could call us dumb and cowardly," Jones announced.

"Why in the hell would you say that? We're not cowards," Schneider argued.

"Oh yes, I am. I cannot sleep at night. I keep having nightmares of being eaten alive by creatures we saw devouring three men. Those were good men that had families like us; we did nothing to save them, nothing at all."

"You're full of crap, Jones."

"Hey, listen to me for a second. It's no one's fault except the man behind all this."

"Yeah, who would that be?" Jones asked.

"His name is Tom Taylor; I already told your partner this. Hey, listen, can we come inside? It's cold out here."

"Sure, come in. Anyone need a drink?" Jones asked.

"I sure could use a drink."

"Schneider, you always need a drink,"

"Yeah, whatever."

After walking inside the vacant house, both men sat on the couch in the living room. After disappearing into the kitchen, Jones returned a minute later carrying a small tray with three glasses of whiskey, filled to the top. After handing each guest a drink, he sat on a lone chair and took a swig.

"Like I was saying, this Tom Taylor, the noted

criminal, is behind the creatures you've seen, I'm sure. I know that he has some magical powers."

Jones smirked. "Tell me, can anyone ever control those creatures we saw?"

"I don't really know if he can control them, but he somehow created what you saw," Jacob said.

"Now I think you're crazy," Schneider announced.

Jacob stood to his feet and said, "Listen to me. There was this ancient wizard named Tobias. He wanted to be immortal. All that was required was to sacrifice a child. Five hundred years ago he did exactly that! I have seen this monster myself; from what I can tell you, he was evil incarnate. I barely escaped with my life. Tom Taylor was his protégé. He has learned well from his master. He is up to something; I only wish I knew what!"

"Why would someone want to return to life if they never died?" Jones replied.

"That's simple. He wants to be immortal. However, that part of the plan didn't work well for the man. I'm glad to report that he was defeated."

Schneider took a drink, set down the glass, and said, "Did this have anything to do with Sterling?"

"It sure did," said Jones. "I remember he had a friend in the department named Jack Danbury. I was a rookie at the time. We all heard of how this Sterling guy helped the mother rescue her kids. But afterward, nothing was ever found of this great Tobias, who they all said was responsible. Shit, man, when it came time to get the remains, all that was left was a black stain on the ground."

"Yes, a black stain," Jacob whispered.

A hush fell in the room; no one spoke for some time.

Schneider said, "Hey, listen, here inside this room, we have three seasoned detectives. If together we can't figure this shit out, then we should quit our jobs tomorrow. It has always been my understanding that evil men want supremacy. If Taylor created these spider creatures, what would be his purpose? What power would he hope to gain?"

"Those things we saw are evil weapons, that much we can agree. So how can we kill them?" Jacob asked.

"Well, all I can say is that they don't have any problem when it comes to killing a mortal man. Look, am I the only one that is scared shitless? I can't sleep at night and have nightmares. Because of this, my wife has walked out on me, especially since I began drinking to get any sleep. I can't function; I never go outside for fear of those damned spiders getting ahold of me," Jones announced.

"You're not alone, pal," Schneider agreed.

"What is the one thing all this has in common, the key to it all? Damn it, I wish I knew. There has to be something that we're missing," Jacob argued.

Jones said, "Earlier you mentioned a family curse. What was the curse, and who did it affect?"

"The families involved were the Bishops and Taylors. It was a curse between them only. Others died in the process, but the fighting between the two families involved just that small group of people. There is something else I didn't mention: Weapons of various types defeated the evil sorcerer Tobias. One was called the Mother's Regret Crystal and the other the Jillian Dagger," Jacob explained.

"Okay, what are these weapons? Where are they now? They have to be somewhere, right?" Schneider asked.

"Yes, I suppose. Hell, I'm not sure, to tell you the truth," Jacob said.

"Are any of Taylor's relatives still alive?"

"I know of one. Heather Taylor, although she changed her name when she got married. I don't remember it. Unlike her brother, I haven't kept tabs on her because she was a model citizen. Regardless, I can find her a person of interest in these murders and issue an APB. It shouldn't be long before we find her," Jacob replied.

"Both she and her brother are connected somehow; she must know his whereabouts, I'm sure of it! Both brother and sister are involved in these murder cases and must be placed under arrest," Schneider said excitedly.

"Hey, wait a damn minute. Did you forget something?" Jones protested.

"Yeah, what's that?"

"We believe Tom is responsible for creating those spider creatures. That guy can harness the power of evil so what chance do we have? Now you want to walk up and arrest the guy and his sister? Don't you think that will piss him off?"

"Who cares if it pisses him off? We have to do our duty as officers of the law," Schneider barked.

"I'm telling you right here and now: Don't do it. Have this Heather woman brought in for questioning and nothing more, I'm warning you," Jones begged.

"Alright, if nothing else you should have this Heather Taylor taken to the station as a show of force, telling her you're onto her," Schneider suggested.

"Who wants to join me?" Jacob said, pulling out his small notebook.

Silence.

The men lowered their heads, staring at the floor.

Jacob, unsure what to do next, sat back in his chair.

"Look, you two. As I said before, I understand your hesitation. Nothing has prepared you for what you saw and experienced that day. Yes, we're all accustomed to seeing dead bodies, the gross remains of car crashes or suicides. But what you saw that night wasn't by the hand of man. In our modern-day existence it's almost to be expected when someone finds their life a ruined mess and wants to end it. But you experienced pure magic; your ordinary world no longer existed. Those creatures should never have existed. Now ask yourselves, should you continue to bury your head inside a bottle or move past it? It's a lot like weeds in your garden. Please don't ignore them when they pop up, and I hope they go away! Evil, gentlemen, needs to be defeated."

"Look, Jacob, you talk a good game. But, man, how do you move past seeing these horrifying creatures?"

"Yeah, listen to him. You weren't there; you don't know what it's like to hear their damn little legs scurrying about the walls, wanting to find a way inside so they can eat you."

"I get it. Really, I do," Jacob agreed.

"Yeah, if only there were a way to erase those memories, our lives would return to normal. That's what we both want. To forget the dreams and nightmares as if they had never happened. Tell me, Jacob, isn't that what you want?"

"Look, I have become a better man because of it. I have accepted that true sorcery exists. Instead of running from it, I have embraced it. Still, after hearing your arguments, I cannot honestly say that maybe, just maybe, there is a way—I mean, a way to erase those memories that you find most troubling. Sure, why not? Magic does exist, and it isn't all evil."

"Hey, now you're talking my language," Schneider said.

"Okay, wait a minute. Let me think about this. Damn, there is an opportunity here. I just haven't asked the right question. Magic, a world of magic, is hidden from us unbelievers. Now having seen it, look at the two of you! Not only have you accepted that a world of magic is alive and well, but you also want something done to remove the memory of it. Who wouldn't? Maybe Heather Taylor can help."

"You keep mentioning her name. Why is that?" Jones asked.

"Well, she is involved. That much I'm sure of. But mainly because the family curse began with the Taylors or directly resulted from something that happened to the family hundreds of years ago. Now besides this, there are other forces at work. There is Stannis."

"Who or what is Stannis?" Jones asked.

"A man or, if you prefer, a wizard of magic."

"Alright, what about him?" Schneider asked.

"Well, if there was a spell—and I'm not saying there is—but if there were a spell that could alter your memories, then this man named Stannis could do it."

"What the hell? Let's do this now. I want my life back, no matter what." Schneider stood up, ready to go.

"Okay, I know a place called the magic store. That's where we will find our help. That's where we will connect with Stannis, I hope."

Chapter 17

SEVERAL DAYS HAD PASSED since hearing the news of her father, Mark. Melissa had not ceased crying as each new day brought forth the reality of his passing. She remembered the tenderness of her father and how he always seemed to know the right things to say when she was facing challenges in her life. To her, his memory could never fade. Forever he would hold a special place in her heart.

After getting off the phone with her sister to finalize a private ceremony for their father, Melissa grabbed some tissues to wipe her eyes. Making the arrangements to bury him was a joint effort. She couldn't do it alone. Rachel, ever resilient Rachel, was her rock, especially when life presented monumental decisions such as their father's memorial.

The house grew quiet with no one around and her two sons in bed. Dan was already fast asleep, having to get up early the following day. After leaving the kitchen, she dragged herself upstairs to check on her sons. After opening their door, she walked into the bedroom. It was dark except for a small lamp burning from the aquarium whose small filtration device hummed softly.

Satisfied that all was well, she turned to leave. After closing the door behind her, she finally glimpsed inside as something caught her eye. Just above Mark and

David's heads was a small blue symbol of some strange design, not noticeable in the light but visible in the darkness.

After walking back into the room, she placed her hand over the light. It reflected onto her skin. Somehow obstructing the image made her son Mark moan slightly. She gasped, horrified; dread overtook her. She knew that powerful magic had been placed upon her sons' lives. Was it to protect them or to mark them for death? How could she ever know?

Desperate for an answer, she raced downstairs to her purse. After taking out her phone, she called Sterling. She got his voicemail. At the beep sound, she excitedly cried, "Sterling, it's Melissa. Please call me as quickly as possible. It's a matter of life and death."

The tears ran down her cheeks. After hanging up the phone, nothing else could be done for her boys. In her sons' room a sinister force had appeared without invitation.

Melissa stared out the kitchen window into the eerie darkness, and loneliness overshadowed her. She remembered her mother and, for the first time, really understood what she must have experienced when Melissa and Rachel were kidnapped many years ago. How strong her mother must have been to face that devil named Tobias. She had even ingested snake venom to search for them spiritually. Apparently, it worked. Recalling that particular day when they saw their mother's mystical incarnation, she remembered how they thought she had died.

The inner strength that their mother possessed would never surrender to evil, especially when it came to family. When Melissa struggled with drug addiction, she discovered again how tough and relentless her mother's love was. She stood beside her, no matter what—even when she stole and hocked her grandmother's engagement ring or pawned the most valuable object that the family possessed, the sacred Mother's Regret Crystal.

When her mother found out what she'd done, she dragged her downtown to find the pawnshop. But she barely remembered the place in her drugged state. After searching the rundown parts of the city, they discovered the pawnshop near a liquor store. When they asked the store owner for the crystal, he explained that an older woman had bought it, asking for it by name.

Barbara wept bitterly when she and her mother left the shop and said, "How could you have done this to our family!" Melissa still remembered the pain at seeing her mother's reaction. From that day forward she vowed never to use drugs again. She has kept her promise even to this day. That was over eighteen years ago.

Now, more than ever, she wished she could talk to Barbara and tell her about this new supernatural sign involving her sons. How would she have reacted? She would have undoubtedly grabbed anything she could use as a weapon, shouting, "Let's kick their butts!" Once again, tears ran down her face as she missed her mother deeply.

Melissa grew tired but still couldn't sleep. She decided to make herself some coffee.

A short time later after returning to her sons' bedroom with a coffee, she sat at their small computer table, remaining vigilant and watching for strange manifestations. The morning hours slowly passed. Soon day dawned. As the morning light filtered into the room, the blue symbols slowly faded, finally disappearing entirely in the morning light and leaving her sons perfectly normal.

When young David awoke he saw his mother observing him lovingly.

"What's up, Mom? Why are you in our room?"

"What? I can't appreciate my handsome sons occasionally?"

Mark began to stir. "What did you do now, brother?" he asked from under the bedsheets.

"Me? I didn't do anything, butthead!"

"No one is in trouble. I just wanted to wish you both a good morning. What's wrong with that?" Melissa asked.

After ripping the sheets from his head, Mark sat up in bed and said, "Really, Mom, it's alright. What's wrong? Are you and Dad getting a divorce? You can tell us."

"No, certainly not. Oh, my heavens, what makes you say such a thing? Your father and I are more in love than we've ever been. No, we're not getting a divorce. Please believe me."

"Mom, tell us. What's the deal?" David replied, grabbing her hand. He looked at her with grave concern.

"Alright, listen to me. Your father and I have always raised you boys to be strong. Do not let life's circumstances drag you down, right? Your grandmother had a saying when my sister and I faced difficult situations. She would tell us, "Be strong and don't give up the fight, no matter how hard it is. Tomorrow will be a better day.""

"Gram said that?" Mark replied, hearing it for the first time.

"I want both of you to be strong for me now, especially since I have something to tell you."

"What is it, Mom? I don't like the way you are

acting," David announced.

"The police have found your grandfather's body; I'm afraid he was murdered."

"What! Grandpa is dead?" Mark cried out. He began to cry.

"Oh honey, I know you and Grandpa Mark had a close relationship. He thought the world of you boys, but I'm afraid he is gone, and we can never bring him back." The words stuck in Melissa`s throat as she began to weep.

Her sons tightly wrapped their arms around their mother as they all wept bitterly. Melissa had known about her father's passing for three days. She just hadn't been able to tell her sons. After seeing the blue light over their heads, it seemed like a good day to keep them home from school and plan the memorial service for Grandpa Mark.

The guest list was short: family plus Susan Bernstein and Heather Taylor Jansen. Afterward, they would adjourn to Melissa's home. Had it only been a few short weeks since they did this for their mother? The pastor, Mr. Hicks, agreed to give the final burial rights at the church. Mark's urn was to be buried with Barbara.

Later that afternoon after everyone had left, the doorbell rang, and David answered it. A stranger stood there: A distinguished-looking man in his sixties had dark skin and wore a black suit and red tie.

"Excuse me, young man, is your mother home?"

David yelled, "Mom, some man is at the door asking for you!"

When Melissa appeared, she happily smiled. "Welcome. Please come inside, Professor Etheridge."

"What a lovely home you have, Melissa."

"Thank you, it's been a work in progress at times, but we call it home. So how have you been, Professor?"

"I'm fine. Oh, you know, the old body isn't getting around as it once did. But still, I manage."

He stopped and took one of her hands. "Melissa, my goodness, what happened to your hands? They're all battered and bruised."

"Oh, that. It's nothing; I have recently enrolled in martial arts."

"Looking at you now. I'd say you were the punching bag,"

"No, I'm fine, Professor, believe me. My instructor requires perfection. He sees something in me that I don't see myself. It's strict discipline."

"I received your package the other day; I was surprised you thought of me. May I ask why me? Why did you feel compelled to send the Jillian Dagger to me, of all people?"

"Is there a place where we can talk?"

"Yes, certainly. Please follow me."

She led the professor into the formal living room and sat near a window. She could see the wrinkles on his face, along with the gray hair. What exploits he must have had in his lifetime. He uncovered the truth in many unexplainable events that boggled the minds of his colleagues.

"You asked me about the Jillian Dagger?"

"Yes," Melissa responded, "I want to know why you gave it to me. Aren't you afraid that I will pawn it? It has to be worth a king's ransom!"

"I find your remark disturbing. Why would you say such a thing?" Etheridge asked.

"You don't know of my past, do you? Years ago, after being rescued from the attempt upon my life, I could not cope with the nightmares and turned to drugs to ease my pain. I sold my mother's most prized possession, the Mother's Regret Crystal, for a few dollars."

"Melissa, I cannot imagine what pain you experienced at such a young age, but I believe you've put that life behind you. According to what Sterling has told me, you've grown up to be a responsible mother."

"Yes, responsible, you say!"

"What is it that has you so upset? Is it the past life that you can't forget?"

"Damn it, could we talk about something other than my past? Sterling helped save both my sister and me from the wizard Tobias. When it comes to magic, I'm done with it having its effects on my life, can't you understand? I don't want anything to do with that business ever again.

"My innocent boys," she whispered. The strange magic in their bedroom still haunted her. She paused, then said, "But why my sons?"

Understanding that something was troubling her, Etheridge asked, "Melissa, earlier you asked me why I sent you the Jillian Dagger. It's because of your father's abduction and death. But I perceive your unwillingness to forgive yourself for past mistakes you made at a young age. Why is that?"

Feeling on the spot, Melissa didn't answer but offered to make coffee for her guest.

They passed the rest of the afternoon in small talk; Melissa avoided anything about her parents or magic. Later David appeared and headed to the dining table to work on his history homework.

"David, where is your brother?" Melissa asked.

"Oh, he's upstairs, playing video games. Why?"

"Do me a favor: Tell Mark he has some math homework. Tell him I said to shut off his game and get downstairs."

Immediately, David ran up the stairs to inform his brother.

"Professor Etheridge, will you stay for dinner?" Melissa asked.

"Oh, I would not impose, thank you."

"Please stay, Professor. The boys will enjoy hearing about your adventures around the world."

"Really, that's cool. You've been around the world?" David asked.

"Actually, I've explored various primitive cultures throughout my lifetime. Often I would find myself in jungles or deserts, searching for ruins depicting the societies that lived before us. However, none could compare to what I've experienced here, close to home."

While walking down the stairs Mark overheard the conversation and piped up, "Was that when Mom and Aunt Rachel were almost sacrificed?"

Turning around, the professor saw young Mark on the stairs. "Why, yes. That's exactly what I meant."

Mark sat down at the table. After opening his math book, he inquired, "Professor, did you ever find any pirate treasure?"

"Alright, listen to me, boys. Please quit bothering the good professor. I'm sure you have a million questions to ask our guest, but that will have to wait until after dinner."

"No, it's quite alright. I always enjoy listening to the young students' questions concerning history. Pirate treasure, you say? Well, I'm afraid that was not what I was after. However, I made a discovery concerning Mayan gold that I believe you will find interesting."

After hearing this, the teenage twins hurried to finish their homework. After dinner everyone retired to the living room to listen to his stories.

The professor discussed an expedition he led to search for Aztec culture and history. Several of the expedition's members had died from cholera, and one died from a fatal snakebite. Still, they pressed on through the dense jungle, hoping to find the ruins of a palace belonging to a young Mayan prince.

He discovered near a sacrificial altar the remains of a tablet. On it were written details concerning the young Prince Cadmael. It explained how he abandoned his family to search for a new location to build a new city for the gods. However, he disappeared into the jungle and never returned.

David quickly asked, "Did you find any gold?"

"No. Regrettably, I contracted yellow fever and barely escaped with my life. However, I can tell you that Cadmael's palace still exists somewhere in the jungle. According to legend, it's filled with treasure reaching the heavens. Any man finding such a treasure would never want for anything. All their dreams fulfilled, they would die happily."

The boys were beginning to yawn, and their mother ushered them to bed, then offered the professor another cup of coffee.

"Thank you, but if it's all the same to you, I would rather have a cup of tea."

"Sure, of course."

After walking into the kitchen, Melissa took a teapot from the cupboard. After filling it with water, she sat it on the stove to boil. After making herself a cup of coffee, she turned to the professor.

"I have to tell you that I've given a lot of thought to

your statement on why I'm unable to forgive myself!"

"You have? That's interesting that you would consider my opinions on the matter."

"Yes, well, the whole thing is in the past, and replaying it in my mind is painful. One does not like to admit that one has a problem. I want to apologize for my outburst earlier; it's completely out of character for me to act so harshly."

"It wasn't my intent to rehash your history. Please believe me."

"No, you're right! I have to forgive myself for what I did years ago. I felt all alone and couldn't deal with the nightmares. My parents were going through a rough patch in their marriage and considering a divorce. Then I turned to drugs."

"Melissa, I can say that you've never been alone in your life. Your mother asked for help from the ones she knew could protect you. It was Stannis who eventually placed a spell of protection around you."

"Stannis, that old guy? No, I find that hard to believe. Why him?"

"Your mother knew that you were in way over your head. Eventually, you would have overdosed from the number of drugs you were taking. What mother in their right mind wouldn't seek help to save their child from themself? It doesn't make any sense not to ask for help."

"Speaking of help, I tried to get ahold of Sterling last night. But he never answered the phone."

"Sterling. Well, from what I know, he's searching for Stannis. I've heard conflicting reports that he has died, but no one knows. May I know why you were looking for him?"

The teapot started to whistle. Melissa hurried to a

cabinet and took a tea bag from a plastic container. She sat it inside the cup and poured in hot water.

"Here's the sugar. Inside the refrigerator is the creamer. If you like honey I have some in the upper cupboard."

"Thank you."

Etheridge walked over and prepared his tea as Melissa took one of her favorite mugs and poured a large cup of coffee for herself.

"Would you like to talk outside? The weather should still be pleasant enough," Melissa suggested.

"Yes, let us retire outside. The view of the constellation Orion should be spectacular this time of night."

After walking outside, they glanced to the heavens and saw the brilliant stars twinkling against the darkness of space.

Seated at the patio table underneath the sky, Etheridge announced, "Do you realize that for centuries humanity has sacrificed to their various gods to appease them—even murdering a virgin young woman and small children of their village?"

"If anyone understands how that feels, it's me," she said ironically.

After taking a sip of coffee, she said, "Professor, let me ask you: Do you believe that Sterling will return soon?"

"Melissa, do you realize you have asked me twice when Sterling will return? What is it that you're not telling me? Why Sterling?"

She began to cry. "Why my sons? They're innocent. Why them?"

"Melissa, why what? Tell me the reason you're so upset."

"Last night when I went upstairs to check on my sons, I saw something I had never seen before. A light emitted from atop their heads, a blueish design that looked like a pentagram or other ancient symbol. When I touched it my son moaned as if in pain!"

"A blue light, you say? Let me ask you: Exactly how big was the design?"

Melissa, sniffling, grabbed her napkin, wiped her eyes, and replied, "It looked like the size of a half-dollar. Does that mean anything?"

"Show me at once. I must see this for myself."

"No, you must wait until my sons are asleep. I don't want to frighten them. I will show you quickly and let you see for yourself."

"Alright, we will wait. Do you have a computer I can use?"

"My husband has one in his study. Both my sons have one in their room."

"Perfect. Can you please show me where your husband's computer is located?"

In the study he sat at the computer, logged into his university, Monarch Hill, and searched for ancient rituals and magical studies.

"Here it is!" he announced.

After clicking on the page it quickly opened on the small screen. He started reading the document aloud, then said, "Mind you, this was written back in the forties after the Second World War by Professor Hansbrough. In his book *The Damned of the Third Reich* he describes a man practicing magical spells as a learned scholar in the occult. Adolph Hitler captured him and co-opted him to his evil purposes."

"What does this have to do with my sons?"

"Look here in this short paragraph. I quote, 'Those

selected for special service or offerings shall wear a sign above their heads as a warning to the spiritual world and dark powers, that the person bearing such a sign is marked for a special purpose.'

"There's more. It says that when an object of magical powers comes in contact with the suspicious blue light, it will change colors to a dark red."

"Let me guess: You're talking about the Jillian Dagger?"

"Where is it? Where do you have it stored? I must see it," Etheridge remarked.

Slowly, Melissa rolled up her blouse. The dagger was in a leather sheath hanging around her waist. She looked at the professor. "No harm shall befall my sons. Do you understand?"

"Yes, I agree," Etheridge responded.

"It wasn't until I saw the blue light hovering above them, then heard of my father's death, that I felt I needed it close to me, just in case I had to fight off a dragon or some other monster."

"I completely understand, Melissa. It's fine with me. Let's visit your sons, shall we? I'm sure by now they're asleep."

A simple nod. "Quick, follow me," Melissa whispered.

Upstairs Melissa quietly opened her sons' bedroom door. After peeking inside, she looked around to verify they were asleep. After giving the okay to proceed, she and the professor entered the bedroom.

After kneeling on the floor, Melissa sat near David's head. Etheridge watched as she quietly removed the Jillian Dagger and positioned it over the fading blue light.

The light suddenly began tracing the blade. Weird

sparkling flashes danced on the sharp edge, and a translucent light blossomed out, covering David in an aqua color from his head to his toes. When she pulled the blade away, the light disappeared.

Looking back at Etheridge, she said, "What in the hell is that supposed to mean?"

Just as he was about to comment, a faint voice called, "Mom, what's that blue light covering David?"

Chapter 18

Sterling was dumbfounded. He glared at the woman and ordered her to look again. "It has to be a computer error."

The woman went back to the screen. "I'm sorry, but according to our records, your friend Stannis passed away about a month ago."

"Can I ask where's his body?" Alexandra inquired.

The woman looked up, wearing a smile, and asked, "Are you family?"

Sterling stood there, unsure how to respond, but said, "No, I'm not, but I'm a very close friend. Together we have fought battles unimaginable to the common person."

Not accepting his friend's death, Sterling walked away, disappointed. He strolled outside and sat on a bench alone.

Disheartened by the news, he stared at the distant horizon. He couldn't believe what he`d just heard; he wasn't sure what to do next. Refusing to accept that Stannis was dead, he stared at the manicured lawn and the park setting with mature trees lining the road. A lone man riding a mower traveled the distance, mowing in a design of his liking. The birds overhead chirped to one another, calling out for a mate. The sun warmed him as it filtered down between the leaves. Finally, accepting the inevitable, a feeling of peace overtook him. He closed his eyes, knowing it would be impossible to fight off Tom Taylor without Stannis.

A few minutes later Alexandra joined him on the bench.

"What does all this mean?" she asked. "Now that your friend is gone and you are alone. Personally, I believe that you left a little too hastily. You should have stuck around to hear what else the woman had to say."

"No, I have accepted too many disappointments to listen further. I expected Stannis to be alive. I can't explain how I can still feel his presence."

"I want to smack you on the head, Sterling. You're such a close-minded individual, probably the most narrow-minded man I have ever met. Tell me, how is it that you're psychic and can read into mysterious manifestations when your mind is so closed off?"

"What, me? Why would you say that?"

"It's because you didn't see or should I say hear what the woman said afterward!"

"What could she have said that would interest me?"

"She told me Stannis was buried in a crypt located in a room beneath a church called The Consecrated Habitation—just thirty miles from here. I'm sure Stannis isn't dead but in a state of suspended animation. Let me ask you, how do you think one could protect themself while recovering from the violence of strong magic? He has to shield himself. What better place than in a crypt, underground?"

The expression on Sterling's face was priceless. He asked Alexandra, "Do you really think it's possible?" Staring back to the horizon to reconsider the situation, he said, "That old fox. It wouldn't surprise me that Stannis had fooled us all."

"Why are we still here sitting on our butts? Let's go get your friend!"

"Alexandra, I could just kiss you right now!"

"Sterling, don't start something you're not willing to finish. I'll tell you what: You can save that kiss for when this is all over. How's that?"

"Sure thing," Sterling laughed. "It's a date."

After leaving the hospital behind, they drove for several hours following the GPS map to The Consecrated Habitation Church. It was well past sunset when they arrived. After walking up to the church entrance, they tried the door. It was locked. Sterling knocked on the heavy wooden door and waited. After several minutes no one answered.

"What do we do now?" Alexandra asked.

"Well, I can only say that I haven't traveled this far to be turned away. There must be someone in charge of this place. Do you see any lights on inside?"

"No, it looks completely dark."

"Damn it! Perhaps I can telepathically contact Stannis from here so he, being the powerful sorcerer that he is, could unlock the doors and let us in," Sterling answered.

Suddenly, two men and a woman dressed in long robes appeared out of the shadows.

"Tell us, who do you seek?" one of the men inquired.

Alexandra advanced, "Your master, the great and powerful wizard of the magical arts named Stannis."

"Are you friend or foe? Speak now," The eldest of the three demanded.

"I have come here to heal your master. Show me where he is being kept," Alexandra demanded.

All three looked at each other strangely, not sure

how to respond.

The eldest member said, "If you are indeed who you say you are, then show us proof or else suffer the fate of the liar's tongue!"

The three apprentices separated and began to wave their hands into the air. A red line connected their fingers and began to interweave a crisscross pattern that grew larger. They spoke a spell in unison: "Hanas, Bravious, Zupa."

After stepping forward, Alexandra opened her purse, removed her two stones, and shouted, "Abaobolus, Gregost, Iumious."

The rocks lifted off her hand and moved toward the center of the red configuration. Blue sparks emitted outward from the rocks, dissolving the apprentices' magical attempt.

The spell was thwarted, and the stones fell to the grass. After reaching down to pick them up, Alexandra placed them back into her purse, eyeing the three disillusioned workers of magic as if to say, "Is that sufficient?"

The eldest responded, "Follow me. I will take you to our master." On the way he introduced himself as Atticus and mentioned that he had been a student of Stannis for several years.

Inside the building they realized it wasn't a church, despite its name. The interior was decorated with several long tapestries and numerous paintings depicting wizards of old. Four large stone tables had been placed to allow members access to various shelves lined by the walls with an assortment of books and ingredients for spells and magic. The smell of burning incense filled the room.

Upon each stone table were cylinders of glass

bubbling atop Bunsen burners, sending off different colored gases that filtered into the room and sending off unique smells, none too pleasant.

More students of magic were deeply engulfed in their studies, busily working on mysterious potions. As the small group walked by, the apprentices didn't pay them any attention as they continued to interpret old books.

Sterling eyed the stained-glass windows around the church and noticed the scenes were not religious depictions as one might think. Instead, they were knights and wizards in battles with dragons and other monsters.

A strange-looking altar was located at the front of the building. It was formed from marble-carved dragons, one black and one white. The white dragon's eyes looked blood-red while the black dragon's eyes resembled bright diamonds; each had a broad jawline that exposed sharp teeth. Their large eyes brilliantly reflected light onto the floor.

Atop their heads were their ears, which came to jagged points. Large claws supported their massive bodies—the tails of both dragons wrapped around an opening in the floor behind them. The opening's surface resembled solid brass, with engravings filled with pure silver on the exterior, depicting various symbols and strange writings.

Atticus slowly approached and knelt as if paying homage to the two beasts. He chanted something in an ancient language as other voices in the room joined in. Soon common rhythmic words formed a sentence. Then something strange happened as the two dragons' eyes sparkled and twitched.

Sterling and Alexandra stepped backward, unsure

of what would occur next. The remaining members came forward to prostrate themselves on the floor as the chanting continued. Slowly, the marble dragons turned their heads and gazed upon the circular opening. The light emitting from both their eyes narrowed and concentrated their energy atop the door on the floor

Next, the different symbols came to life, displaying various strange colors. A round image of colored lights appeared in a transparent display that began twirling over the opening. Whatever was inside was protected by powerful magic.

The sound of mechanical locks being disengaged was heard. Soon the dragons' tails began to move. As they drew inward into their bodies, the brass opening on the floor also moved, disappearing into the unknown depths. A platform began to rise upward until it locked in place, flanked by a staircase made of fine brass, with steps leading down into the abyss.

Atticus stood to his feet while the other wizards were still chanting. He turned to Sterling and Alexandra and said, "Please come forward."

Without hesitation, they joined him at the stairway.

"Come, I shall take you to Lord Stannis."

They descended only a few steps when Atticus lifted his hands and said, "Zipesidus, Hazaon." Torches mounted on the walls ignited. The brightly shining space exposed a long stairway before them. They followed it downward at least three stories into a cavern. The musky smell in the cramped room meant that little or no air ever penetrated the sealed tomb.

They walked farther into the cavern, finally reaching a room that opened to the large corridor. The walls and ceiling were decorated with symbols matching the ones upstairs. The roof curved to meet the walls some twenty feet apart.

In the distance they saw an ornately carved granite table. Lying upon it was the body of Stannis. As they approached, they saw a bright canopy above him. He didn't move or acknowledge their presence but remained unconscious, staring upward into the unknown.

Atticus turned to them and said, "Here lies my lord Stannis."

"How long has he been like this?" Sterling asked.

"He's been like this since he battled the other sorcerer and lost," Alexandra said.

"It is as she said," Atticus replied.

"So is he in a coma or what?" Sterling asked while examining his friend.

"No, he's in a protective state of self-awareness between the earthly bonds that will end his life and the magic that keeps him alive. He's not dead," Alexandra explained.

"The magic projected to keep him alive is beginning to fade as if the dark forces that struck him have grown stronger. What assaults him now is the continuation of the dark magic that he fought. Something has to be done to save his life or he will die," Atticus explained.

"I have seen this event in my past visions," Sterling explained.

Turning to Alexandra, he said, "You must save him; you're his only chance for survival."

"I know this, and yet I'm afraid. When dark magic is undone, you must realize that the creator will become aware of who it is that has unraveled his efforts. He will become furious. That is why I'm hesitating. Yes, I realize that it is my destiny. Sadly, if I'm to die, then so be it."

Atticus added, "I owe my master everything. If this is our only chance to save his life, I am willing to lose my life in the attempt."

"I regret that we are ill-equipped to perform this spell to save Stannis," Alexandra said. "I should have realized this before we came here, but I had no idea what sort of spell it was that imprisoned your friend. There is one missing component, something so valuable, I really doubt that we can obtain it. But without it, we cannot save Stannis."

"Tell us what you need," said Sterling. "If we can find the item, we will."

"I'm afraid you're mistaken, Sterling."

"Tell us," Atticus said while stepping forward.

She looked dismayed. "Please listen, the key to saving Stannis is the rare blood of a Taylor child; the younger the child, the purer the blood. It was a Taylor who issued the curse, and Taylor's blood has the power to break the spell."

"What in the hell are you saying?" Sterling demanded. "You're going to sacrifice a child to save Stannis? I refuse to be part of this."

"Sacrifice a child! Stannis would never allow it, even if it were meant to save his life," Atticus objected.

"Good Lord, that is not what I'm saying at all. We just need a drop of blood, not to kill the child. However, to my knowledge no such child exists."

Shaking his head, Sterling seemed nervous. "You're wrong. There is one."

"That's great news."

"No, I'm not so sure," Sterling turned away. "How can I ask this of one particular mother, Heather Taylor? What if she refuses?"

"Simple, Stannis dies," Alexandra replied.

Acknowledgments

Creating a book requires the hard work of dedicated people. I especially thank Karen Hodges Miller at OpenDoorPublications.com for her tireless efforts in editing and arranging the book details in proper order.

I thank Mat Yan at M.Y. Cover Design for making the book cover. Great job, Mat.

I also thank Lisa B. Snyder at silverhoopedge.com for designing the web page for my books at https://timothypatrickmeans.com/.

About the Author

Timothy Patrick Means was raised on the sunny beaches of Southern California. As a young boy, he spent many summers swimming and playing in the ocean without care. He worked for many years at McDonnell Douglas on military aircraft and, most exciting of all, rockets! He learned about all types of space hardware, including the space station, space shuttle, and the Delta rocket.

He is the father to four children and two stepchildren, and a grandfather to fourteen.

"I've always loved writing," says Tim. "My first experience at being creative was describing my feelings through poetry, which I did with mixed emotions. But it wasn't until I put pencil to the paper to write fiction that my imagination soared, and I was set free to explore all the possibilities of creating an exciting story."

Tim has published several books and has more in the works. Along with The Bishops' Resolve Series, of which *The Bishops' Struggle* is the first of three books, there is its prequel, The Bishops' Sacrifice Series, a group of three books. He has also published *The Sterling Chronicles,* which further explores the adventures and mysteries of psychic detective Sterling, as well as a series about pirates told in the classic adventure style of *Treasure Island.*

www.ingramcontent.com/pod-product-compliance
Lightning Source LLC
Chambersburg PA
CBHW070356200726
48294CB00003B/943